A Very Inappropriate Affair

Tales of Loyalty and Infidelity

LISETTE SKEET

Strategic Book Publishing and Rights Co.

Strategic Book Publishing and Rights Co., LLC
USA | Singapore
www.sbpra.net

For information about special discounts for bulk purchases, please contact Strategic Book Publishing and Rights Co., LLC Special Sales, at bookorder@sbpra.net.

ISBN: 978-1-68235-317-2

Author's Preface

In the real world, people in relationships make mistakes. They say or do things they later regret, and often wonder what possessed them at the time.

I have shared study groups for subjects which include psychology (forensic and observational), psychodynamic theories, person-centred theories, and more. In my experience, the exploration of such topics gives rise to much debate. Some individuals can be very frank.

"I don't know why I did that!"

"I wish …"

With counselling training, and the skills of motherhood which build as children grow, I have reflected on many aspects of upbringing and outcomes. In psychological analysis, it's possible to understand and recognise natural character traits, and inevitably, to examine to what extent a person's behaviour is affected by their history.

My fictional characters make their mistakes. I wonder if readers will judge them harshly, or find it possible to engage in the stories, and try to understand how events and actions came about.

PART ONE

Marisa and Jack

Marisa

Marisa was a "surprise baby", born to her parents some years after they gave up any hope of having a family. They were unimaginative people, living quietly in a comfortable home in the Essex countryside. It was fortunate they were open to offers of help, and they were not offended by a concerned health visitor who saw they needed advice in the early days of Marisa's life. However, they kept the baby safe, clean and fairly well-fed, and continued kind enough, just about, as she grew.

In a scenario that could have led to adoration and spoiling of a precious child, these two coped placidly, accepting their lot, and harmless in their intentions. Yet, in some ways, they were neglectful.

Perhaps they would have been surprised to know there was more to parenting than meeting a child's basic needs. Marisa was a good-tempered child but her mother's solution to her occasional fractious times was simply to place her inside a playpen with a few toys. When she grew too big for such confinement, she was often supplied with books and left to her own devices. It was fortunate for Marisa, that the modern use of the internet was yet to come. Her developing brain was protected from the effects of a brilliant screen, and, after all, she was secure, and her mother was never far away, only placidly knitting in her chair, or pottering around in the kitchen.

Time passed and both parents would have been surprised by the idea that there should be greater efforts from them to cherish their precious child, to help her achieve her dreams and to bring pride and happiness into their lives too.

Marisa's father worked as a counter assistant in the local post office. Charlie was an unambitious person. He earned enough money to keep his small family fairly comfortable and always refused promotion, although it was repeatedly offered. His hobby was gardening and he owned a sizeable piece of land, which he divided into neat squares and apportioned them with precision, to lawns, vegetable plots and flower beds.

In summer time, Marisa was allowed on the lawns only to walk, or sit down to read her books. There were no games of rounders, hide-and-seek or "catch" in the immaculate grounds of the family's detached home.

Her mother, Brenda, was a quiet woman. She kept house and took in extra washing and ironing for a small personal income, although there was little evidence of the way in which she spent the money. She worked through tasks laboriously, taking roughly twice the time a more energetic person might have needed. Always cordial to her customers and to neighbours, she was generally solitary, and did not seek activities outside her home life.

The family lived in a property bequeathed to them by Charlie's father, and they knew nothing of poverty.

* * *

By the time Marisa was ten years old her mother was fifty-three. Anything but dynamic in her youth Brenda, unchanged, was settling into relatively idle middle-age.

Although no harm came to Marisa when she was growing up, in some ways she suffered. The delight felt by most parents, even in the smallest achievements of their children, was absent in Charlie and Brenda. Extra classes or hobbies outside school were not a part of the child's life since, if she asked about swimming or gymnastics clubs, or music lessons, her interest was dismissed. Her parents couldn't see the point.

Marisa's winsome appearance was taken for granted and since no-one praised her for the way she looked, she was uncertain about how she compared with other girls. Generally, she wore her long, light brown hair in a tightly woven plait.

She was given new clothes only rarely. Brenda could well afford to pay the prices in the stores but she had a love of bargains and clothed herself and her daughter with items from the charity shops. Marisa longed to choose garments for herself, especially as she entered her teenage years when she would have loved to make modern choices that would suit her.

"This will do for you, Marisa!" Brenda was proud of her ability to hunt out bargains.

How wonderful, Marisa thought, to wander along rails full of new clothes, knowing she could buy something. She dreamed of thick, new coats with silk linings ... neat, fitted trousers ... pure white shirts that felt crisp to the touch (not limp, from being steamed in some stuffy back room), and sweaters in flattering shades of peach or toffee.

The family ate regular meals, but their food was plain. Her parents were not interested in cookery and they would never have considered the nutritional value of the dishes. At thirteen years of age, Marisa was somewhat thin and it was a direct result of insufficient food as her young body began to develop. Her mother seemed unaware of her daughter's normal changes. She never arranged for school dinners and simply wrapped a few sandwiches in a parcel, with a chocolate wafer or some fruit, to sustain her during the hours from eight o'clock each morning, until four in the afternoon.

Every Sunday, at roughly midday, the family ate a roast dinner. It was the main event of the day and they did little else. During the morning, Brenda used a sharp knife to scrape fresh vegetables in a bowl of water placed on her knees while she listened to the radio, basted the roasting joint of meat occasionally, and finally created a good meal from modest ingredients. It never occurred to her to engage her daughter in cookery. She had no thoughts of enhancing the food in any way, and Marisa had no idea that it was possible to make vast improvements to roasted meat with a variety of different sauces.

Except for rare trips to the seaside in summer, the family spent their life mostly in their own narrow environment. Marisa developed a habit of studying on a Sunday. To while away hours after the family's main meal, she carried her leather case full of books and papers to her room, spread everything over the patchwork coverlet on her bed and selected pieces of homework to address, steadily working through each subject, one after the other. It was a way of passing the time and she was quite lonely, but the hard work served her well in school and college later.

Marisa would have dearly loved a modern bag made of denim or lightweight cotton, such as those her school companions slung over their shoulders so casually; however, her mother ordered school supplies and selected an old-fashioned briefcase with careless disregard for her child's preferences. Footwear was chosen for hardwearing usefulness and Marisa was provided with narrow leather shoes which she wore, unquestioning, with no change of style for many years.

If the weather was fine, homework could be tackled out of doors, where she could sit at a picnic table carefully placed in the exact middle of the terrace. There were neatly folded rugs in the airing cupboard, and sometimes Marisa collected one to spread out on the springy mown grass. She hunted for clover occasionally, running her fingers over the lawn's surface, hoping to find a stem with four leaves, but while vivid green moss was embedded in places, both clover and daisy stems were cut so short, they couldn't be spotted in the grass. Narrow flower borders around her glowed with colour; bees hummed above the blooms, and there were always pigeons, cooing in the tall trees that surrounded the garden. When sprinklers were switched on, Marisa had to respect the watering process and remove herself from the lawns.

Marisa extended her study hours at the weekend and there was no reason to curtail them. Charlie took a nap after Sunday lunch before switching on the television. Brenda rested too, peacefully sleeping away the time until four o'clock, when, with a heavy tread, she made her way to the kitchen to make tea and sandwiches. She loaded a tray with this teatime meal and carried it into the sitting-room, where she set it on a low table, then took her own plate of food and settled comfortably again in her armchair with the special footstool nearby.

Largely ignored by a family who fostered no great ambitions for themselves or for her, Marisa stayed childlike for longer than some of her peers. In the quiet home where friends were not encouraged to visit, she applied herself to her education, even though praise never came. It was a dull life for a child, but tolerable, the only one Marisa knew and she was fairly content. Like many neglected children, Marisa did not long to be somewhere different, despite sometimes being aware that a few changes would be welcome. The absence of any form of lively interest in her character and ideas was something she was too young to identify.

Mercifully, Marisa was allowed to decorate her bedroom exactly as she wished. This led to a fascination with wall paints, fabrics and soft furnishings, as well as a love of colour, and all these interests grew as she improved and developed her own small environment.

Brenda found cushions and curtains in charity shops, but she preferred bedclothes and bathroom linen to be acquired first-hand. This meant, when Marisa had a birthday, or at Christmas time, it did not matter that Brenda lacked ideas, Marisa could ask for quilts, pillow cases and throws in the colours she loved. She took pleasure in a fluffy white blanket for extra warmth, or a brand-new bale of bright yellow towels to stow inside her tiny en suite bathroom. On occasion, a request for a new sweater or a skirt *was* granted on a birthday, and her mother's musings over "value for money" didn't spoil the pleasure for Marisa.

In school, since there was always awareness that others could be less fortunate than herself, Marisa did not feel particularly disadvantaged by her uninspiring family. A classmate had a father who drove her terribly hard to succeed in everything she did, whether it was academic or sporting. The child suffered from anxiety and bit her nails so relentlessly, the fingertips were raw.

Another girl had a mother who always looked as if she had materialized from a magazine cover; yet she was seldom at home and placed the child in the care of a nanny, not only immediately after school ended each weekday but also during evenings and school holidays. The woman was far more interested in her own achievements than those of her daughter. Marisa's mother cared little for her daughter's progress too, but at least she was in evidence, calmly knitting or watching the television in the evenings. Marisa learned that occasionally, if she sat at her mother's feet to watch television, the woman would lay a gentle hand on her head, in the merest acknowledgement of affection.

In primary school, she was quickly identified as "very able", and by the age of ten, "gifted". Marisa's parents were sent letters to this effect, but although they dutifully filed everything along with school reports and certificates, if they understood such information to be significant, there was no evidence of it. Life at home went on as before.

Thankfully, the school's headteacher took a special interest in such a promising student, gave her extra books and prompted her to analyse texts, and to be reflective. Marisa enjoyed creative writing. She wrote stories, in which the central character bore similarities to herself, but lived a charmed life as a fortunate person who was extremely happy. In these fantasies she always made her heroine "very pretty", which was a vision of perfection she did not think she would ever achieve.

Her studies and personal determination to do her best served Marisa well, and she qualified for a grammar school education. She liked the atmosphere of the orderly school. The ethos there was overwhelming for some students and nervous upsets were common – especially during examinations – but Marisa benefitted from certain guidelines which were missing from her home life. She certainly maintained a daily routine with her parents, and that aspect of school life felt familiar, but for many hours at home she was left to her own devices. In school, every part of the day was organised, and there were even severe restrictions on how one spent the break times.

With the disinterest of her parents, there was one useful effect on Marisa. They had no high expectations of her. No-one was actually sarcastic about what she could or could not do, and no one ever deliberately decried her achievements. Marisa was sure of her ability to study effectively. She passed tests, behaved impeccably and was polite to her classmates and teachers, all of which resulted in her appointment as Head Girl when she was seventeen. It was an honour which she tackled a little shyly, and to the best of her ability, and she was surprised but encouraged when Charlie and Brenda learned of the award and finally showed a certain solemn approval!

Marisa addressed A-level examinations with the same sensible determination. She was heading for university and it was not difficult for her to pursue this ambition although inevitably she had to apply for places, attend interviews and secure a student loan all by herself. With no rejections, she deliberated over her location, picked a university in the north of country, and there found pleasure and comfort in the company of similarly well-motivated students.

CHANGES

Aged eighteen, Marisa abandoned a habit of years when she began to loosen her hair from its tight braid, and let it cascade down her back in shining coils. With her gentle femininity increasingly evident, she earned the interest of a boy or two, and if she had seemed introverted to begin with, there came a change. In a group, especially when they discussed their studies, Marisa could appear confident; becoming animated she found her voice and was encouraged when others listened. Yet, she was still intrinsically shy. Confronted with a boy who was interested in dating, she had a tendency to blush, and struggled with a problem known to many shy people: the more they redden, the worse they feel!

She engaged in a couple of sessions with a counsellor within the university, and would have been glad of some useful advice. Instead, there came the baffling information that her shyness was a form of vanity. The counsellor was a very young woman herself, and her words sounded as if they were regurgitated from some text she had read only recently. Marisa felt suspicious, couldn't trust her and didn't believe the theory in any case. She abandoned the therapeutic process, so-called. She would work on her self-esteem in her own way.

Personal pride developed naturally since she continued to pass examinations, found herself well-respected amongst her peers and, increasingly, attracted admiration for her obvious prettiness.

At the end of the semester, Marisa returned home and was not unhappy, feeling glad of a break. She unpacked books and files in her familiar bedroom, which her mother had prepared for her return with attention to spotless cleanliness but no artistry. Marisa picked a few tall daisies from the garden when her father's back was turned, found a spare vase beneath the kitchen sink, and set the modest bouquet on her dresser. She had some new clothes bought with her student loan, and she hung them inside her wardrobe where an old duffle coat and a couple of tartan skirts still graced a top shelf. A collection of fragrant toiletries, as well as a few daring items of make-up, also adorned the glass surface of the dresser. Content, she settled there for the long summer holiday.

Charlie and Brenda showed fractionally more interest as their daughter began to develop her own life and over the Sunday dinner table, at long last, they paid her some attention. They had been dull parents but they were not bullying, and now they became quite deferential. There had never been any sarcasm or spite throughout her childhood to spoil her perceptions and Marisa could make what she would of the world around her.

Marisa obtained her degree, and after two or three dull internships (where she was shamelessly overworked) she made up her mind to find a job that felt worthwhile. She planned to live near her workplace and rid herself of the draining daily commute from her parents' house. Before long, she found her niche in publishing and fell quite naturally into the work of editing and proof-reading. She rented a couple of rooms on the top floor of a narrow town house and enjoyed her own space, which she filled, typically, with comfortable furnishings, flowers and books.

* * *

Marisa was becoming a confident woman who felt able to express her feminine nature. She bought pretty things for herself, and felt attractive at last. Developing a glamorous style, she perfected her make-up, chose a potent signature fragrance and from the same expensive range, collected bath oils, talcum powder, body lotion and colognes. She liked clothes in soft fabrics and on her slim wrist she wore a heavy silver bracelet, to which she regularly added extra charms.

The routines of the publishing house seemed burdensome after a couple of years, and with only mild regret for a familiar daily life alongside a handful of good-natured colleagues, she removed herself and began to undertake private editing. This meant she continued to earn an income for something she enjoyed and had the added bonus of freeing her from an imposed routine – now, she could please herself and organise her time exactly as she wished.

For years, Marisa had been essentially a loner, who made no significant friendships. In truth, she was afraid of them, having few experiences of forging a real connection with another person. Her classmates, then her work colleagues, had respected her but generally left her alone since she gave the impression that it was preferable. Her solitary life was renewed in some ways, now that she worked privately, seated at her own desk in her flat. She had learned how to be resourceful and there was comfort in familiar patterns with precious freedom to plan each day exactly as she wished, but her life was, once again, too quiet for a young woman.

Marisa awarded herself a free day sometimes, and she would seek out a park, or visit local places of interest. In an occasional call to Brenda, she chatted about her health, and that of her parents, or the weather, or Charlie's garden projects. Brenda was not the kind of mother who enquired into her daughter's activities in any detail. An onlooker to Marisa's life at that time, would surely have wanted to encourage her to address her loneliness. Following a minor decision, in fact she managed to make a change for herself.

* * *

Marisa ran to the top of a flight of stone steps, which took her to the entrance of the public library. On a paved, semicircular area, she paused. Nearby, was a slim woman, who was clutching a sheaf of papers in one hand and, with her free hand, trying to guide a small boy who very much wanted to go a different way. Marisa bent to pick up a wafting page, handed it to the woman, and pushed the door of the library open.

"Come on Austen," the child's mother encouraged him, and they followed Marisa inside the building. "You can choose some books to take home!"

There were volumes from a well-known children's author scattered on a low table but the boy turned his back on them, and went to a low shelf to make his selection. Once he seemed to be giving the books his attention, his mother joined Marisa at the counter. They waited, side-by-side, while the assistant's attention seemed to be fully taken by a whirring printing machine.

"He won't have anything to do with those," the woman observed. Marisa glanced towards the child, then back with raised eyebrows. His mother was fiddling with her hair, adjusting and re-pinning a smooth blonde knot, but she indicated the garishly illustrated books which her son had rejected. "The stories turn dark. He's only ten. He gets upset ..."

Marisa had never interested herself in the series for children, although as an editor she was aware of the popularity of major authors. Most of the work she edited was academic and beautifully written. She thought Austen's preference for uplifting tales was understandable.

The counter assistant abandoned the printer at last, and in response to queries from both ladies she began to hunt for brochures and flyers, bending to examine the contents of shelves beneath the counter.

Marisa had made up her mind to learn a little history, having been bored by the dullest teacher imaginable during her schooldays.

In fact, it was a subject in which she had failed to shine, after struggling to memorise endless dates and giving up, more or less, and only scraping a pass in the exam (much to the surprise of her classmates!)

"I know someone who is doing a psychology course," observed Marisa's companion, apropos of nothing in particular. "It's making her really miserable!"

Marisa remembered how utterly useless her therapy sessions at university had been. She liked this dry comment, and she chuckled. Soon the two women were chatting. They took their brochures and sat together at a low table, not far from Austen who was sprawling comfortably on a bean bag decorated with pictures of caterpillars.

Marisa confided her interest in aspects of history she had found wanting at school and her new friend, whose name was Julia, revealed her ambition to be a life coach. Would she need to study psychology? Marisa wondered, but Julia thought not. She described her intention to be a positive influence in the role; she had researched, and there was no need to get a degree for life coaching. She was determined not to dwell on people's past lives and times – instead, she would look at aspects of their lifestyle and help them go forward. Marisa was impressed by her enthusiasm.

Julia was a few years older than Marisa. She affected a slightly knowledgeable air about most things they discussed. Thus, in the way of "best friends", she became someone to like and lean on, but – on occasion – she could be maddening. She was lively company. After that first meeting, often the two women walked together to see Austen into school before they went on into the town centre. He always ran across the playground without complaining, was immediately enveloped by a group of friends, and never looked back. Julia said she was relieved that her son liked lessons, and Marisa, watching the tussle some parents were experiencing as they tried to persuade their youngsters to go through the tall iron gates, was not surprised.

She walked on with Julia and if the morning was fine, they collected coffee in plastic cups and made their way to the park, where they chatted about many things. It was a term-time routine they both enjoyed. About their online courses Marisa took a genuine interest in her friend's life coaching. She found she had to be philosophical about receiving less enthusiasm from Julia for her expansion of ideas about history!

Julia was happily married. She lived in a different world, in a way, and Marisa toyed with the idea of envying her. She wasn't positive that she did – although, surely, it would be lovely to have someone faithful and supportive in one's life? Marisa enjoyed her independence.

So, with a friend whose company was enlivening, and as a certain youthful glamour continued to develop, in her late twenties Marisa enjoyed life and her confidence grew. With style, a toned figure and an appealing, heart-shaped face, she attracted male attention. She accepted some dates but had a fairly pessimistic view of the likelihood of a long-term outcome. She was not inspired to spend significant amounts of time with any man.

* * *

Marisa enjoyed companionable chats with Julia over coffee or, sometimes, a meal. They rarely touched upon anything deeply affecting, and generally she kept her innermost feelings to herself. She enjoyed and completed a short course on the subject of World War II, was fascinated and saddened, and then set aside thoughts of extra study as she took on increasing amounts of editing work.

Julia's interest in advising others was important to her, part of a bigger plan which she had resolved to stick to. She elected not follow a possible natural path to overlap with subjects such as psychology or philosophy. Marisa, who occasionally interested herself in her own responses and actions, was so self-possessed that she never offered her sensitive private thoughts up for challenge. Feelings of isolation could be alleviated by an inspiring routine and planning interesting times to look forward to, which still held joy because of the long days of her childhood when she was forced to stay endlessly at home. She joined clubs, including reading groups as well as energetic activities such as swimming and aerobics.

Occasionally, she would visit her mother and father, who continued to enjoy fairly good health as they moved into their seventies. Perhaps it was because they had eaten so lightly? Neither of them carried any excess weight. However, Marisa took gifts of food treats which she hoped they would try.

She also selected toiletries for her mother, choosing those with a light fragrance. For Charlie, she collected gardening magazines. Her offerings were received with polite thanks. It seemed the gesture, at least, was appreciated and Marisa was touched on one occasion, when she entered her parents' bedroom to fetch a cardigan for Brenda and saw the bath oils and soaps neatly arranged on a dressing table, and the glossy magazines, stacked by her father's side of the bed.

She always professed to admire the lawns, which were still immaculate, and stayed on for a day or so, until she felt she simply must flee.

PIERS

Marisa bought a bungalow as soon as she could afford a mortgage, and began to give her imagination free rein. Living in the outskirts of the town now, she would create a home she loved. By the age of thirty, she was a fully independent woman. She dressed in casual clothes often, but always presented a feminine, attractive appearance with her glossy tangle of long hair and creamy skin.

She enjoyed making herself glamorous for an occasional evening out, and on being invited to a party in a London hotel something spurred her to make a special effort. The event was arranged by the agency that supplied most of her work. Marisa chose to wear a classic little black dress, fine stockings, high-heeled shoes in a silky shade of caramel, and delicate touches of silver at her ears and neck in addition to her bracelet. She looked stunning with a smooth, upswept hairstyle.

The party was unremarkable, although there was plenty to drink and a tempting buffet spread out on tables covered with gleaming white linen. Faintly bored, Marisa took a slice of Brie and some grapes for her plate, then weakened and added a wedge of treacle tart. She made polite small talk with other guests, finished her fruit and cheese, and waved away the waiter who proffered a tray of glasses filled with champagne. A voice nearby commented, "Who sends away champagne?"

17

Marisa turned and saw a tall man, who regarded her with brilliant blue eyes, then held out his hand. "I'm Piers ... and you are?" Marisa shook hands politely, and said her name.

"Wouldn't you like some champagne?" he asked. "It goes well with treacle!"

Marisa smiled. Perhaps a drink would help her to relax? "Well ... maybe ..." She wasn't sure that she would be able to eat a sticky dessert in front of a stranger. Her old shyness loomed.

Piers followed another waiter, collected a glass and carried it carefully back to where she stood. He moved with athletic vigour. She liked the way he was smartly presented in his expensive suit and shirt, and thought he looked like a model, with a lean frame, angular bone structure, and classically smart dark hair.

Piers had a flattering manner of giving all his attention to Marisa as soon as they began to talk. He listened carefully when she responded to the usual questions to describe her job, and her interests. In her turn, she asked a few questions. He was expressive when he spoke, with expansive gestures of his arms and hands.

The room was filling up with guests and at last Marisa laughed and shook her head in response to a comment from Piers – it was impossible to hear his words clearly. He placed a guiding hand on her back, and they moved away from the crowds around the bar, past small circular tables where couples were sitting to eat, drink and talk, and went outside onto a balcony, where the sound of music was muted. The dark night sky was full of the pinpricks of stars, a garden below was mostly in gloom but there were fairy lights strung in nearby trees. They were not alone but the few couples who had also escaped out-of-doors were chatting quietly.

Holding their glasses but taking only occasional sips, Marisa and Piers talked as if they would never stop, mainly about their careers, but also finding some common ground, for each was the only child of older parents. At last the evening ended, lights began to be dimmed and they walked through the deserted function hall and went down thickly carpeted stairs to the reception rooms. Guests were shrugging themselves into coats, and leaving through the revolving doors. Piers was reluctant to leave her, and he didn't attempt to hide it. Suddenly overwhelmed by this turn of events, Marisa said she must make her way home but she would see him again. She collected her lightweight coat from the concierge, Piers held it for her to slip into and, in a little gesture that felt unexpected but kind, bent to turn up the velvet collar around her chin, observing that she should keep warm.

They walked across the hotel forecourt. Several taxi cabs waited at the side of the quiet street, their roofs gleaming under street lights, and Marisa headed for the car at the front of the queue. Piers courteously opened its door and held it while she climbed in, then he stood back with an expression suddenly devoid of levity. They had already exchanged their phone numbers. He didn't move to kiss Marisa, or even speak again, but she knew he was struggling to let her go.

The driver peered into his rear-view mirror, then accelerated away from the kerb. Marisa sighed, leaned back in the leather seat, and knew she was deeply tired. Somehow, she could still smell the scent of Piers' expensive cologne. She wondered, fleetingly, what became of her plate with its half-eaten slice of treacle tart. She knew she had finished her champagne and then – despite animated conversation – another, and now the alcohol, the excitement and an overwhelming sleepiness were catching up with her.

* * *

Piers had a dignified charm, and at the age of thirty-six, of course, he was aware of it. However, he was deeply respectful and Marisa liked him. She accepted his invitations, although she made sure of her own input when dates were arranged. She was careful not to seem too eager, but they went out to dinner, to the cinema or theatre at first, then, as their friendship developed and quickly became a romance, sometimes they were happy simply to wander. They chatted, window-shopped and eventually shared a table in some snug coffee shop or bar.

When Marisa suggested they might drive into the countryside and find a river walk, or somewhere they could picnic, Piers was happy to agree. He was enthusiastic about walking and Maria had to admit, he set a fast pace!

Marisa enjoyed the time they spent together. She became accustomed to his company, his classic style and the cool scent of his cologne, and soon found that he admired her too, not only for her beauty but also because of her lively intelligence.

Since they were both lucky enough to have money at their disposal, they made the most of exploring a variety of restaurants, sometimes challenging one another to try some new dish but always returning to their preferred Chinese food before long. Marisa knew she let her mind wander just occasionally when Piers mentioned his work. (Linked to shipping, somehow … was it just a little dull?) She knew how to seem to be paying attention and also, how to change a subject. Yet, there was really nothing wrong with their relationship, for Piers was besotted with Marisa, and they inspired each other. It seemed they were able to remain animated and friendly, even when they disagreed.

Almost six years her senior, perhaps, just occasionally, Piers was too close to being paternal in his manner. The subject of marriage came up but not with any drama. They mused sometimes about their compatibility. Such detached consideration was somewhat separated from emotions. Piers felt frustrated when Marisa would not marry, especially as – despite all the vocabulary she had at her disposal – she could not satisfactorily explain why she refused. It was certainly wonderful to be cosseted and treated in a way she had never experienced before but nevertheless, their four-year relationship ended because Marisa didn't think she could carry on, honestly, in such a close relationship. Piers was regretful and even annoyed, and yet, somehow, they retained their mutual respect. They cared about one another, and occasionally they spent a few hours together on a deeply friendly basis.

Julia was still apt to assume the air of an older sister. She liked Piers, and she was reproving. "You could have been happy with him!" It wasn't helpful. Marisa knew she would have been *safe* with Piers ... but happy? The point was, she wasn't sure.

"Now, the way you are going on, you might end up never being a mum!" Julia mourned "... and you are so clever and gentle, you'd be good!"

Never having shared her childhood with brothers or sisters, Marisa could not imagine herself with a baby. Her mother had also been an only child, and Charlie – who had grown up in care, for reasons he never explained to Marisa – seemed unaware of any siblings or a wider family, so there were no cousins for Marisa to play with, when she was very young.

For some people, a lonely childhood leads to an absolute determination to create a family with companions for the first-born, but Marisa's upbringing lacked maternal warmth and it was something she had neither observed nor truly experienced. She possessed both good humour and compassion; however, perhaps inevitably but certainly for the time being, she was coolly focused upon herself.

* * *

A year passed, then another and new habits overtook the old. Marisa thought about Piers often; he wasn't left behind in her past. She tried to understand her feelings and began to see that she still felt a great liking for the man. He made her feel feminine, was attentive and generous. Marisa wondered if there was something wrong with her! Why had she been so sure they hadn't a future together? Doesn't a sense of security lead to happiness? It was an interesting idea because, after all, she was the product of a secure, yet relatively unhappy childhood. Developing the train of thought, although

Marisa saw the comparison, she nevertheless acknowledged that Piers was nothing like her parents, reserved souls that they were. He was enthusiastic about keeping her company, making her happy, and showing her how much he would cherish her ... so (Marisa reasoned) the problem definitely lay within herself.

Things began to change for Julia when her son went away to university, where he would stay in student accommodation. She, herself, was about to move house with her husband and would live some twenty miles distant from Marisa's home. Their friendship had run its course in a way, and despite a certain fondness for one another and promises to keep in touch, they weren't unduly upset by their separation. Marisa had begun to think she was the one who did most of the listening, during their meetings. As Julia was freed from active parenting duties by Austen's growing maturity and independence, she altered and seemed less empathetic. A hard-working and practical person, somewhat strident in her manner, Julia could make disparaging comments about the choices of others. Such remarks were more frequent and Marisa guessed that she, herself, could be a target for her friend's unwelcome criticism!

Mostly, Marisa was back to being on her own in her pretty and beloved environment. A dozen gleaming koi carp swam in a well-tended pond, set below rockeries in her garden. The fish were well cared-for, along with her lawns and flower borders, by a mild-mannered, elderly neighbour named Derek, and he was paid a small amount for his time and careful work. He lived a quiet life with a fragile, ailing wife, and Marisa knew he valued an occasional, friendly conversation.

Patiently, Derek created a garden Marisa loved, with sloping lawns curving at the edges instead of being cut into sharply geometric shapes. There were water plants with delicate fronds, splashes of colour in beds full of dahlias; rockeries where daisies were in abundance with forget-me-nots and grape hyacinths each spring time. An apple tree, past its youthful glory, still bore an abundance of sweet, ruby red apples in September.

The old man proved very kind whenever Marisa felt down-hearted. He was free to enter the kitchen if he needed items such as a clean bucket, or something from the collection of small tools which Marisa kept in a cupboard beneath the sink for such times as she, herself, felt like a spot of gardening.

"I've got that sharp little fork, Marisa!" he would call out, and she didn't mind, because he was conscientious, and she knew he would clean and return the tool.

He had a knack of noticing when her work kept her for hours at her desk, and would make a welcome appearance in the doorway of the study, carefully carrying a mug full of steaming tea, which was dreadfully dark but gratefully received nonetheless. At such times, before making and bringing her drink, he prudently covered his muddy boots with a couple of carrier bags, tied at the ankles with string. Marisa tried to get him to weaken her tea once but his solution to this was the generous addition of extra milk, so she gave up and accepted the strong brew he favoured.

She liked his calm, kindly manner and while he had no clue as to what she typed as she endlessly corrected and revised manu-scripts, he was nevertheless admiring of her skills.

Marisa accepted her renewed, mainly solitary state, neither par-ticularly enjoying it nor wanting to change so much she would grieve for Piers' company. She even let him take her out sometimes, knowing he could be trusted and would not pressure her to change.

Julia stayed in touch with occasional calls and emails but her life coaching kept her busy, so, for much of the time, Marisa was alone as her mid-thirties approached and although typing in her small study was reminiscent of her childhood isolation, now she could manage her lifestyle as she pleased.

* * *

Marisa continued to live in her bungalow. After almost seven years, during which time she spent most of her personal allowance for luxuries on her home and garden, she loved her environment more than ever.

Inside, there was cool and stylish comfort. Rooms were decorated in neutral shades of cream, fawn and taupe with some walls painted silky white and an occasional artful dash of a deeper tone, such as the orange carpet in the hallway and the navy-blue cushions fastened to the seats of kitchen chairs. Furnishings were a combination of modern and traditional, with a collection of mismatched chairs for the scrubbed pine kitchen table, and a cottage suite in the airy sitting room, where a floral print was echoed in the curtains.

On a whim, Marisa bought a four-poster bed. It took up most of the space in her bedroom, but she loved to draw filmy curtains around it, indulging in fantasy, sleeping beneath clean white cotton sheets and a light duvet, with a thick blanket on top, if she felt cold.

She ran to the corner shop for the occasional treat such as chocolate, a pot of yoghurt, apple juice or wine – or if she was out of something essential. The women who served there were always rude. After having been a faithful customer for so long, Marisa thought it would be lovely if they said "Good morning", or addressed her directly instead of looking away when she asked a question or – at best – answering casually. She positively disliked their attitude, but she was used to it and this semblance of resentment barely touched her consciousness, as a rule.

Was it because she was pretty? Marisa was no longer oblivious to this. Or were they very bored, and envious of her relative freedom? It didn't matter … not then.

JACK

With her thirty-fifth birthday imminent, Marisa found it was, not surprisingly, a significant milestone. She taxed her mind over her reluctance to marry Piers but inevitably came up with the same conclusion. There *was* no good reason for her to refuse him, he was lovely! She simply valued her independence, and maybe there was something missing from the relationship when they were together. Marisa had few experiences with which to make a comparison but the answer to such a recurring quandary was simple, after all. She needed to feel sure of real love in her own heart, before she would make a commitment.

On a Friday evening, casually dressed in jeans, sneakers and a blue fisherman's jersey (which was a size too large for Marisa) she went on foot to the little shop.

In the store, she chose a bottle of wine and placed it near a till. There were no other customers and for the moment, no evidence of anyone to serve her, so she wandered around, looking unhurried, probably, but feeling faintly annoyed by spaces on the shelves despite cards which proclaimed bargains. There was supposed to be a special offer on muesli, but there wasn't any muesli. At length, tired of such a waste of time, Marisa took a carton of milk from the cold cabinet, returned quickly along an aisle to the counter, placed the carton alongside her bottle of white Merlot and fished inside her pocket for her purse. Would she get served? It was time to escape!

Marisa hadn't bothered to comb her hair. Her curls were glossy, and she was fragrant with perfume, but her tendency to indulge in casual dishevelment had grown worse since she separated from Piers. She pushed a stray curl out of her eyes with the heel of her hand and regarded, with solemn brown eyes, the young man who emerged from another room. He wore an overall over his clothes. He came to the counter, where he faced Marisa.

"No muesli?" she asked, only slightly hopeful that a packet would be produced.

"Muesli?" He raised dark eyebrows, as he unlocked the till.

Marisa opened her purse. "I expect it's all gone ... I wanted to get that two-for-one!" He apologised in a straightforward way and she smiled, pleased with his unexpectedly decent attitude. "Well, it's not your fault!" she told him, noticing his hazel eyes had irises rimmed with black.

The next time Marisa shopped; the young man was waiting for her when she arrived at the counter. She was in her typical hasty mode and she rarely delayed once she had picked up everything on her list, but it was impossible to miss his expectant air. "Did you see?" he asked, looking directly at her face. This was a novelty in itself; there, where the mostly female staff were usually completely disinterested in their customers.

"What? See what?" she answered and started to smile. He was charming; the wide grin was infectious.

"What I did?"

He was all lit up! Marisa thought, but she regarded him composedly.

"What? *What* did you do?"

He pointed. He had tidied and stacked boxes of muesli in the correct place and secured the special offer card immediately in front of them. She collected two packets and returned to the till, laughing.

"Thank you!" She had spotted a hint of mischief in his eyes, and responded to that gleam, remarking inconsequentially, "Everyone likes muesli!" She could guess what he'd say, and was right.

"You know what? No, they don't!" He shook his head, grinning.

Marisa tapped her card on the machine, and observed that he should probably set his sights on being a manager. She was charmed again when he shrugged, shyly.

After their brief exchange, Marisa fell into the habit of chatting with the young man. She asked his name and he indicated his badge. "Jack". She spoke the name, still being faintly maternal. Unexpectedly, he said he had seen her before, but Marisa was bewildered by this. "Where was I?" she asked.

He explained: he knew Julia's son, Austen and used to wait for his friend to walk with him into school. He said, "I think I remember seeing you at the school gates sometimes!"

Marisa wondered why this piece of information gave her a small sense of shock. It was quite a coincidence, for one thing. Inevitably, it also brought into sharp focus their difference in age. "I'm sure you don't!" she answered, a little too fast, feeling abashed in her turn.

Their interest in one another wasn't harmed by the revelation that, not only had they crossed paths before, but also, they did so from two completely different standpoints. They could make each other laugh, and it was fun. The simplest of chats became worth the effort and developed into shared ideas. If there were no customers queueing behind her, Marisa lingered for a few extra minutes after she had paid for her groceries.

She did not analyse this new acquaintance and merely thought Jack was a personable soul. Perhaps she would get around to telling Julia about him, some time? He had ideas comparable to Marisa's own, in a way. He wanted to move on from the shop and go travelling, and he spoke about visiting places she was interested in, so she described her own plans and some similar ambitions. They liked live bands, and discussing gigs they found they were both at the same one a few months before. "Well, I didn't see you!" Jack said, making her laugh, considering they were both lost in vast crowds of people.

* * *

Jack had the widest of grins. His eyes sparkled when Marisa walked into the shop and he confidently greeted her. He would confide if he felt tired after a long day. He told her when he booked an appointment for a new tattoo. "Last year, I got this ..." He extended an arm and rolled up his shirt sleeve to show her. "I wish I hadn't, now!"

Marisa inspected the depiction of a dove, and brief, curly lettering .... *Coco.*

"Someone's name?" Again, a little shrug. She waited. He straightened his sleeve. "Did you go off her?" She bit her tongue then, because the question was too frank. Also, she was to question herself later, for it did not occur to her just then, that a girl might go off Jack! How could anyone help admiring those mile-long lashes?

"Yeah. She was ... Oh, well ..." He frowned down at his sleeve, rebuttoning the cuff. "It's a bloody stupid name too! The guy at the tattoo place is gonna make it different, put in another picture and cover up the writing!" Respectfully, he added, "He's a genius!"

Getting tattooed was one of the least likely things Marisa would do, ever, but she listened and said nothing critical. Already, it was as if they knew each other very well and they shared a happy, funny, casual friendship which neither one of them would wreck. Increasingly. Marisa looked for Jack and found she was disappointed if he was not on his shift. They seemed to be soul mates; they really did. However, it was not a situation she pondered over, and she didn't mention it to anyone else.

A Spider and a Shock

In the shop, Marisa was nearby when an elderly man reached up to take a bottle of wine from a high shelf and his action disturbed a huge spider, which moved fast then stopped, clinging to the cardboard packaging on some beer bottles. The young assistant gasped. She ran out from behind the counter and disappeared through the doorway at the front of the shop.

The customer hesitated, frowning down at the screen of a mobile phone. "It doesn't matter," he commented. "My wife just told me she already bought some!" He hurried out of the shop, leaving the wine bottle on the counter beside the abandoned till.

Marisa, who did not share the horrified reaction of the shop assistant, counted change in her palm. The woman made as if to creep back inside the shop, keeping her distance, pressing the heel of her shoe against the door to hold it ajar. "Don't you like spiders?" Marisa asked, unnecessarily.

"Oh, I'm really scared of them! My mum always hated them too ..."

Marisa's mother had never reacted to a spider or beetle, and Marisa had spent hours lying on her tummy in the garden, watching the activities of tiny insects. She had no reason to be nervous. "*If you want to live and thrive – let that spider run alive!* Do you want to get a cup and a piece of cardboard? I'll get him out for you!"

"Huh," the assistant let the door swing shut. She supplied Marisa with a mug and a strong brown envelope then dragged a set of steps near. *"Ugh!"* She went to wait outside the shop, where she lit a cigarette, no doubt feeling the minor scare was worth it.

Marisa climbed the stepladder, and lowered the mug over the spider, which had shifted just a little and was now motionless beside a bottle of Chardonnay. It seemed just as well the assistant hadn't seen the creature move again.

"Are you okay, up there?" asked a familiar voice. Marisa needed to concentrate and it was immediately difficult with Jack behind her, but she expertly slid the envelope underneath the mug which, upended, trapped her prey. With both hands engaged, when she turned around, she wobbled. Strong hands grasped her waist and a voice full of laughter asked again, "Alright?"

Maintaining as much dignity as she possibly could, Marisa had to let him steady her until she landed safely on the floor, where she looked up and met his beautiful, hazel eyes. Cautiously returning, the shop girl did not spot the way Jack and Marisa were looking at each other. She gave them a wide berth, skirted the wine shelf for good measure, and hurried back to her till.

* * *

The month was April, and the weather was variable. As a dull day darkened and evening drew in, Marisa heard raindrops drumming hard against the windows. She glanced at the numbers in the corner of her screen … 17:54 … then shut down her computer, stacked papers, pushed back her chair from the edge of the desk and stood up. She moved around the bungalow then, to light lamps and close curtains. The rooms soon looked cosy but her solitude felt overwhelming.

Marisa had coping strategies for such times. In her kitchen, she turned dials on a radio and found some music. She switched on a kettle, spooned instant coffee into a small white cup and enjoyed the fragrance when the boiling water was added. In a few moments, a generous handful of pasta was tipped into a pot full of bubbling water, and began to cook.

Marisa shook a little brown sugar into her cup, then, absently stirring, she stood at the window looking at the sodden garden lit by the soft glow of outdoor lights.

Feeling lonely … warned the part of her that missed Piers.

I'm not! argued her independent self.

She turned away from the window, and regarded a pile of laundry despondently.

At length, deciding to get on with tasks, she sorted the heap of clothes. They could be put in the tumble dryer after the wash. Marisa thought she would go around the house to tidy up, and in doing so she would make herself feel uncluttered and better! Once her household was in order (she made herself a promise) she would have a glass of wine.

She reduced the flame beneath simmering *fusilli,* added a pinch of sea salt, then chopped a courgette into generous pieces and prepared to pan-fry a piece of chicken. With the utensils, the oil and meat set out, before the next steps in her cookery she collected an umbrella from the stand in her hallway. For both washing powder and the wine she would have to make a dash through the rain to buy supplies.

The shop continued to be poorly managed and shelves were frequently cleared before the end of each week, with customers asking hopefully, about their chosen items, if there was "any out the back?" They were rarely lucky enough to be told, there was.

Marisa could see, as she stepped back, the brand of washing power she wanted was there, but just one super-sized packet remained, pushed well back from the shelf's edge. She had no hope of reaching it. She raised an experimental arm then immediately felt silly. She would have asked for the footstool but when she hesitated, she saw Jack coming to her aid with his typically buoyant stride.

With a mental flashback to his expression after the spider rescue, suddenly, Marisa caught her breath. "He is so young and happy!" she thought. His presence beside her was powerful, putting the remnants of the bleak day behind her in the nicest way possible when he smiled and she felt warmer somehow, watching as he easily stretched a long arm to grasp the heavy box, which he took to the till for her.

"Merlot?" he asked, turning to the wine shelves.

"A mini one," she answered hastily, and saw a gleam of amusement in his eyes.

A Compliment

There was an early heatwave in May. Flicking through the pages of a magazine one evening, Marisa made up her mind to wear her hair shorter. With the idea still appealing the next day, she popped into a salon and got a trim, thinking she would feel cooler. Although sometimes she pinned her hair up, Marisa had never worn it loose above her shoulders before and when she went home and examined her reflection in her bedroom mirror, she decided it looked surprisingly nice. She dipped her fingers into a pot of styling lotion, ran them through the shorter layers and let the curls spring into a bouncy frame for her small face.

Jack, whose dark hair was cut close at the sides and left heavier on top, was enthusiastic. "Your hair's great!"

Flattered, she enjoyed the compliment, but she was used to being admired. Pretty women have every right to make the most of their good fortune! She might have thought little of it, except … there were knowing looks being aimed their way from the shop assistants, directed first at herself then Jack. Were they resentful, in that unpleasant way of envious women who lack a generous spirit? What were they thinking?

An uncomfortable possibility occurred to Marisa! Surely, they didn't think she would *flirt* with Jack? She got a faintly uneasy feeling and tried to dismiss it. Perhaps she imagined some kind of attitude, from them … but it proved impossible to forget those smug expressions.

* * *

In defiance, Marisa continued to use the shop occasionally, but it got harder.

Jack was certainly a confident person, especially considering his youth, but his natural way of chatting with Marisa disappeared. Despite feeling incredulous, sadly she believed it – there was a big change. He was diffident but still worse, he appeared to be on his guard. He did not meet her eyes and this proved so painful, Marisa tried to avoid looking up at him when she paid for her shopping. This awkward situation continued, until one day when, glancing up from the contents of her purse, she caught him in a disconcerting stare from beneath those endless lashes.

Acutely aware that there was no mistaking a difference in Jack's attitude, she was careful to be polite although she found her heart ached in a way. They had fun in a fleeting but genuine friendship. So many people are unfriendly … these human connections are sometimes what make life worthwhile! Could Marisa ignore the problem, whatever it was, now?

Regardless of her efforts to pare down her conversation to the minimum, before long there was a ridiculous grin from the young-est shop assistant, an interested stare from the older manageress, and it was impossible to dismiss the perceptions they had. With an uncharacteristic flash of temper, Marisa found herself hesitating on the pavement before leaving. Her heart pounded. She set her bag on the ground and half-turned to go back as she contemplated marching up to the women and yelling at them! She wanted to jump on someone's toes, make them pay for her embarrassment. Instead, too sensible after all, she forced herself not to create such a scene. She would walk away, for Jack could be the person to suffer if she did something "over the top" like that.

On the short walk home, Marisa's thoughts whirled. In a way, she was baffled. How on earth had this misunderstanding arisen? Considering things in a different light, trying to adopt a viewpoint of a bystander, she remembered all their animated talks. Neither one concealed happiness upon seeing each other and Marisa saw that her new haircut was the sort of thing other women might attribute to attention-seeking.

She wanted to tell poor Jack to ignore the staff and their rudeness, but found she didn't know how she possibly could. How could she risk highlighting that mutual interest between herself and Jack? It would be very uncomfortable, especially as he was effectively trapped. With respect for his right to feel comfortable in his workplace, Marisa thought perhaps she would have to keep away. She could choose her routes and actions, whereas Jack, confronted and feeling awkward, still had to serve at the till. Marisa knew how it felt to be shy.

* * *

When she was alone, Marisa ate lightly. During her childhood, her diet was often bland. Now although she consciously sought interesting flavours, she ate salads and fruit, wholemeal bread and foods which could be cooked quickly, such as omelets or fresh tomato soup. Sometimes she bought goats' cheese or feta with olives; often she preferred not to bother to make a hot meal. She didn't rely on food as a form of comfort and her interest in cookery all but disappeared, when she was solitary.

Eating out was enjoyable, and of course she missed spending time with Piers. A restaurant meal in his company had its appeal, but they were officially separated. She would not chase after him since she knew her decision had caused him pain, and for his part, he did not contact her every week.

Marisa liked to order most of her shopping online, it was so easy to purchase the bulk of her groceries, as well as clothes and home accessories. Nevertheless, when the work of editing manuscripts was arduous, she would become forgetful and slightly scatterbrained. It was not unusual to tear herself away from her computer at nine-thirty in the evening feeling bemused by the passage of time since she first sat at her desk that day. Wandering into the kitchen, she was apt to find no milk, and no filling for a sandwich in her refrigerator. At such times, she would run to the corner store, which stayed open, fortunately, until eleven o'clock at night.

On the way there, jogging to stretch her legs but mentally still caught up in her work, she often reviewed an excerpt from the documents with her mind still full of complex detail.

Marisa went to the corner store for occasional treats, when she bought oddments such as notebooks and pens, a newspaper, some chocolate or a drink. At other times, she collected essential items when they were needed ahead of her next online shop.

After considerable thought about the shop girls and Jack, Marisa realised she had some awareness of his shifts. She began to use the place again but tried to avoid the times when she suspected Jack would be there. This was annoying but – determined not to be over-faced by foolish gossip – she put aside thoughts of fun and chatter, reasoning that she encountered plenty of different people who potentially enriched her life.

One afternoon, after collecting a packet of chocolate caramels, a carton of cinnamon yoghurt, and a magazine, she returned to the bungalow with plans for a piece of writing filling her thoughts, and found she was out of milk. Marisa disliked black coffee. She dumped her bag on a table, retrieved her purse and ran out again with a checklist of urgently needed extras forming in her thoughts.

"I forgot a few things!" Marisa hurried into the aisles again, making her comment to no one in particular. A woman continued to stack new items on shelves, ignoring customers. A couple of children took ice creams to the counter, paid another disinterested assistant, and left the shop.

As she gathered her shopping together and saw Jack coming to take over till duty from a girl, it seemed obvious this second set of groceries was comprised of essential items. Marisa had selected milk, brown rolls and a box of tissues and she found herself acutely aware that, perhaps, most people would not have forgotten those and made sure to get them on the *first* shop?

An assistant, who knew nothing of absent-minded erudition, had stopped looking disinterested and instead, was staring. Did she think Marisa purposely separated her shopping so that two trips were essential, hoping to see Jack on the second visit? Or that she had become forgetful due to an infatuation with Jack? Neither of these thoughts were very likely, Marisa knew. She was becoming sensitive, and far too anxious! Of course, the assistant probably just stared blankly!

Absolutely furious with herself for guessing, Marisa recalled her plan not to let rude stares matter at all, but she became embarrassed and counting change turned into a task that made her feel foolishly over-faced.

The shop emptied and Jack's assistant was called to help with filling shelves. Marisa's cheeks flushed. She felt the creeping warmth, hated it, and trembled, praying he was unaware. As she tipped money into his palm, their hands touched. It was the merest brush of skin on skin but her thoughts went into startled confusion.

"It's only me!" Marisa told herself silently. She scooped her groceries in a careless motion into her bag. "Must be! It's me who has this – this *feeling!*"

The milk carton was crushing a loaf of new bread and she pushed it aside, then looked up, to find Jack was watching her. His expression was thunderstruck! She raised her chin and gave the faintest shake of her head, then shouldered the bag, headed for the door, and fled.

HONESTY

At home, Marisa scattered her purchases across the worktop. She found her sweets, grabbed the packet and opened it. Eating, she was trying to treat herself to ease her distress; it was something she rarely did. She turned, and leaned her back against the kitchen unit, thinking hard.

By now, Marisa had come through many social trials, and she was confident person. During her university days she had discovered how lively she could be. She made no significant friendships at that time, but was well-respected nevertheless; she knew how to be pleasant – distant, yet inoffensive and good natured. Without the shackles of a certain depression which had affected her in days long past, when her mother was always quiet – sometimes seeming downhearted – and her father's ways were subdued; through the years Marisa had managed to build on a fundamental self-possession. Despite few guidelines for forming relationships, her natural empathy and high intelligence served her well.

A child who cannot be sure of their parents' approbation may grow into a deeply uncertain adult but Marisa had risen above the dull days of her youth, even though she continued to be selective about forming bonds. She was very different from the uncertain teenager she had been, different even from the young woman in her early twenties when her femininity was slowly developing. Real self-assurance had come late. Now she possessed it, but surely her responses to Jack had only been motherly?

"If I know what I'm doing nowadays ..." she wondered, "... how come I went into *that state?*"

* * *

"What's your name?" she had asked kindly, and smiled when he told her, "Jack" and raised a shoulder because it was written on his badge.

Jack is barely out of school! The narrative began in her thoughts.

Marisa made coffee and carried it into the garden, where she sank down onto a stone bench and raised the steaming cup to her lips. With her free hand, she absently stroked the friendly tabby cat that slid through a broken slat in the fence, coming to lean, purring, against her legs.

She remembered how attractive Jack's first grin seemed, and the way his eyes lit up when he spoke animatedly, to explain something that interested him. He was thin – too thin really – but he was very tall, broad-shouldered, and he had a certain presence. He dressed immaculately. His hair was cut close to the sides of his head and left in masses of dark curls on the crown. How would a teenage girl see Jack? Marisa teased her brain.

"Rather nice" she thought, because of that devastating smile! Now she faced it, Jack was good-looking, and she admired his style. Thanks to judgmental people and an inevitable train of thought, her eyes were opened.

Had those gossips spotted something that was *true?* This was not funny! She would have to hide, surely? Conversation and laughter, life's plans expressed in just a few sentences? They were – or should be – all over.

With an impatient gesture, Marisa put her empty coffee cup aside, letting the dregs spill into the short grass by her feet. She felt saddened, and angry. No-one had the right to make her feel embarrassed but she was certainly in an awkward position. If she tried to grab her shopping and rush away, would she look guilty? (This, she reflected uncomfortably, had already happened, and perhaps she had offended Jack too.) If she attempted to chat, there would be more insinuations. She wanted to be fair: the shop, such as it was, was Jack's place of work. It seemed a definite decision was in order – she really had to keep away!

In the early hours of the next morning, Marisa woke up in a tangle of bedclothes, having dreamed of an intense scenario which involved Jack and went dreadfully out of control. She got up, and went to the bathroom to splash her hot face with water, then made her way to the kitchen to switch on a kettle and make a cup of tea. She carried her tea back to her bedroom, but sleep was lost.

By four o'clock on that cool morning in early summer, she sat in the window of her living-room, clasping her mug, looking into the garden where she could see only shapes until dawn slowly crept in. There were the tall reeds in the pond, the pretty garden furniture and the neighbour's striped cat, sitting on the low stone bench to wash.

Marisa was deliberately reviewing everything that happened so far, as well as her dream and its intensity. She worked out the age difference more carefully. Aloud, she exclaimed, *"Oh, God!"*

* * *

Days passed. The soft, light feel of early summer disappeared with the beginning of June, and each sunlit day stayed warm as it slipped into evening. One week since Marisa had bought anything other than online groceries, having run out of milk, she contemplated her options. She never used her car for brief trips, and was not about to change this. She had always been happy to walk the short distance to the corner shop. Suddenly, the bother of trying to go elsewhere and leave Jack in peace seemed annoying!

Restlessly, she turned away from the refrigerator, where she had been staring at a blank space while she wondered what to do.

"No, I *can't* be bothered!" she exclaimed aloud. She hunted for a hairband in a drawer and twisted her hair into a curly ponytail, then slung a pink pashmina around her shoulders, chose comfortable trainers and left the bungalow.

Gleaming in the twilight, the lights at the shop's front came into view and Marisa stopped walking, torn for moments by new anxiety. Her shoulders slumped a little, in an unconscious expression of indecision, and she stood still, trailing her wrap, and her empty shopping bag. Then, with both thoughts and pashmina gathered, she went on, meaning to rush hastily on. The pathway would take her downhill, and in ten minutes she would arrive at the garage and buy her milk there.

In the gathering gloom, further on from the glow of lights, she saw a familiar figure and it was impossible to run past. She hoped it did not look as if she actually skidded to a halt.

Jack was leaning against a wall, flicking a lighter which he held to the tip of a cigarette. Crinkling his eyes against the smoke as he exhaled the first drag, he looked directly at her with a nod, and – yes – there was his grin. He pushed himself away from the crumbling red brickwork with an elbow and straightened up. He snapped closed the lighter and pocketed it.

"They can shove it, the whole lot of 'em. I've left! I got out ..."

"You left?" Marisa echoed.

"Yeah!" He trod on a cigarette butt; he must have been chain-smoking. He didn't expand any further. She watched him brush a speck of ash from his dark jeans, and straighten a shirt cuff. He was immaculate, as always.

"Well ..." Forcing herself, Marisa made as if to go on, turning towards the brow of the hill and the track ahead.

"Wait," Jack moved quickly, put a hand on her arm. *"Marisa!"*

It was the first time he had said her name. She heard his voice, heard the urgency in the sound; but it was a sound that felt like a caress.

An Ending and a New Beginning

At the start of her affair with Piers, Marisa fell in love with him. He had charm and perfect manners; the way he loved to treat her to gifts and outings was enticing … and he had movie star good looks.

They spent a long weekend by the sea in Devon, where hot weather and lovely surroundings enhanced their happiness. On the first evening, after sharing a shower with him, Marisa was ready to go out for dinner looking suntanned, and faintly haphazard, with her curls, blue jeans and a flowered blouse. She slung a short denim jacket around her shoulders and they went off to get their meal.

In a dimly lit bistro, they sat close together near a window, sharing simple dishes – crispy French fries, a quiche and salad, sizzling hot onion rings. They poured rough red wine into balloon glasses, and remarked on its rawness but enjoyed it, nonetheless.

When they were ready to return to their hotel, Piers stood up and held the back of Marisa's chair as she followed suit. He took her jacket from a peg near the doorway and helped her to slip it on, then solicitously buttoned it, smiling into her eyes, reminding her of a similar gesture on the night they met.

Their relationship became a fact and they were happy. Friends began to accept them as a couple, and invitations to parties or other people's weddings were addressed to them both. Piers did not move into Marisa's home altogether, he kept his town flat because it was near his workplace, but every weekend was spent in the bungalow and their routine was fixed. Derek began to consult with Piers about the garden. Julia was used to hearing Piers' voice if she called on the land line. Once or twice, they went together to visit Charlie and Brenda, ate dinner, and spent a quiet Sunday afternoon, and Piers knew how to chat to the elderly couple without making them feel overwhelmed by his sophistication.

In retrospect, Marisa was not sure exactly how she came to end their relationship. Of course, it was the long and increasingly hopeless wait for her agreement to marry that spoilt things for Piers. By that time almost four years had passed since they first met, and although Marisa still wandered about in some sort of dishevelment occasionally, she made herself glamorous for their outings. That way, she reflected Piers' own style.

On a still summer's evening she wore a short dress of cream linen, which flattered her slender brown legs and left her shoulders bare. Her hair was smoothly straightened and wound into a coil on the nape of her neck. They went on foot, along a familiar route through the little town to their favourite local restaurant where they ate an expensive meal, with a starter of rich pate followed by lobster and a green salad. Everything seemed as lovely as before, yet, somehow, they entered into a discussion and a review of their time together, and the conversation did not go well.

As they walked back to the bungalow, they were not arm-in-arm. Piers had plunged his hands deep into the pockets of his loose jacket. Marisa carried a little bag over one shoulder and had her fingers tucked into the strap; her other hand she, too, pushed into a jacket pocket. They tried to talk, but no thread of conversation would flow happily, instead the expression of discordant feelings went on.

Marisa could not say she would marry. She had to hunt for a tissue in her handbag, dabbed her eyes, tried to remove smears of mascara from her cheeks. Piers could not look at her and his jaw seemed set with a certain obstinacy. With neither of them the sort of person who wanted to become heated or angry, they slept, side-by-side, worried by their unhappiness. The following day, sadly, he left.

* * *

Having stayed Marisa with his touch, Jack crossed the narrow pathway to take her by the hand which he held in a firm grip, all the way down the sloping path to the garage. He did not speak and raised the cigarette to his lips a few times. His profile was enigmatic. Privately she fought her nerves, despite a powerful sense of glee.

In the garage store, she collected a container of milk. Jack bought cigarettes, chocolate and crisps. Like a schoolboy with a crush, after they left the shop, he handed her a bar of caramel chocolate; and yet, with eyes brilliant in their intensity, again he halted her with a hand and his words. There was nothing childish about him. Before she ran back to her home, he asked her to meet him the next day.

* * *

Jack wanted Marisa to wait for him in the park. Dressed in a loose and fragile summer shift dress, with her hair brushed and framing her face, wandering slowly alongside flower beds ... scented, day-dreaming ... *she did.* When he appeared, striding purposefully through the open gateway, grinning, her heart lifted. He carried coffee in two tall plastic cups. He indicated a seat with a nod and she went to join him.

Together on a smart new bench, disinterested in the inscription on its shiny brass plate, they stared into each other's eyes and felt their revelation unfolding. Shameless in confessing how they felt, not with words but with body language, they discarded empty cups and tightly held hands, both hands, clasped in Marisa's lap.

Talking, they charmed one other, and were funny again; but nothing that was happening seemed childish. He met her eyes respectfully, but he leaned towards her, so their faces were very close. When a honey bee settled on her shoulder, he brushed it from her skin and she followed the gesture with an involuntary movement of her own hand.

Marisa stopped being stunned and felt excited again. She could barely believe what was happening, for here it was – the truth! Jack desired her and the feeling was mutual. It was an experience quite different from her early meetings with Piers; she was not wooed – unless she counted the chocolate bar! She was seduced by their mutual attraction.

In his speech, Jack was laconic but, in his manner, so very focused, he was anything but idle. He was fascinating her and drawing her in. Her soul was willing. He looked down when she shifted her position, crossing her legs at the ankles. The flimsy skirt of the little dress skimmed her suntanned knees and he moved to draw the tip of his little finger softly over them, picked up the hem of the fabric and held it between slim fingers. It was hard not to tremble.

When Jack asked if Marisa would like to meet him the following evening – maybe sit outside a pub, and talk again – she began to go for the idea without a care. Distant chimes of the church clock could be heard and somehow, they intruded on her thoughts. She hesitated. She shut her eyes. "Maybe!" she said, although her heart called out *"Oh, yes!"*

"Maybe?" Instantly upset, he insisted: *"Look at me!"*

Marisa raised her chin, saw his serious expression, the softness of his beautiful wide mouth as he fell silent and waited for her to reply. He was sensitive. She murmured, "I'm not sure …" She was thinking about how others would perceive them, and it was a worry she could not dismiss.

Jack stood up. He regarded her reproachfully for a moment, then turned and began to stride off. Frightened and hating to see him walk away, Marisa had a sense of impending loss. "Oh no …!" She started to run.

He heard her quick footsteps, and stopped walking as she over-took him. He saw her spin to a halt before him and waited, with his head inclined fractionally on one side. She hesitated, just a moment with her arms half-raised, then slipped them around his slim waist. Wordlessly, she drew him against her, rested her cheek on his chest and stood still, holding him. Felt the pressure of his arms as they came round her, his hands as they were buried in her hair.

"I'm not a kid!" he said, fiercely. She looked up and could not reply, for at once he was kissing her so hard, she couldn't speak. "I don't care about anyone else," he said when at last he drew back. "I … like *you!*"

"Yes." Her mouth burned. She would be a fool to reject him.

"You know what's going to happen, *don't you Marisa?*"

THE WAY SHE WAS

Marisa liked to wear nail varnish in shades of peach, mocha coffee, hazelnut or pistachio. She rejected modern beauty gurus, and her gleaming nails were not matt but glossy. She was a small woman, with softly curling caramel-coloured hair. Her brown eyes, dark-lashed were apt to gaze on the world solemnly but at times they lit with humour. Her narrow hips might have lent a boyish appearance but she had a voluptuous bust. The fronds of pale hair curled around her neck, and she wore a heady perfume. There was no mistaking her feminine charm.

The following day passed slowly for Marisa. Before they parted, Jack had asked her again to meet for drinks the next evening; she agreed and having faced her feelings, it was hard to wait.

The day wore on, Marisa was self-indulgent and set aside thoughts of working at her desk. She spent a long time on her appearance, gradually completing all the small preparations that make women feel sure of themselves. She spread out favourite garments over her bed, then found herself tossing them about, trying to decide what to wear ... chose grey silk trousers, loose fitting, and a white lace top that dipped low at the front. At long last, incredibly, she stood before her mirror, dressed, perfumed, and glowing with fresh make-up ... and excitement. A final spray of hair lacquer, and it was time to take her narrow purse, leave the bungalow, lock the door, and seat herself in the cool interior of her car. She switched on the ignition, glanced at her reflection in the rear-view mirror, and set off.

Jack was waiting at a local pub, where a sign bearing a depiction of a pheasant hung at the entrance to the car park, motionless in the still air. As soon as she crossed the threshold, Marisa could see him standing at the bar, grinning in response to a comment from the bartender. His hair, with its deliberate waves and the frond, glossy with gel, that fell against his forehead, was flawless. He wore a grey jacket, gathered on the cuffs and on his narrow hips. Tight black jeans. Dark leather boots with a pointed toe. From the corner of his eye, he spotted Marisa and turned away from the bar, and his grin grew still wider.

They carried drinks outside to the garden, found a table where they would feel private, and settled themselves under a willow tree by a river. Marisa had a single glass of wine and followed it with lemonade. She had driven there deliberately, determined not to let alcohol cloud her judgment but as for hanging on to any sense of reality or normality, it was a lost cause. Jack, with his wonderful wide grin, his long stride as he crossed the public bar to meet her at the door, and the warmth of his presence at her side as they made their way towards the river, had taken her breath away. She was faint with longing for his arms to encircle her again.

* * *

They sat opposite one another on low wooden benches, leaning their elbows on the picnic table. Jack studied Marisa's face, then reached out to touch a tiny pearl cluster which she wore on a fine chain around her neck. "I like … this …" His fingertips brushed her throat.

Conversation was easy, revisiting subjects they had shared before the shop assistants began to stare. Jack seemed relaxed when he talked about music. He was more confident than ever; again, Marisa considered that he had none of the awkward self-consciousness that seems to plague very young people. His reticence, when it appeared after the staff were rude must have been at odds with his character, brought about, perhaps, by conflicting feelings. (Perhaps they had gossiped in front of him.) He was drawn to Marisa but respectful of her relative maturity. However, he *was* self-aware and his appearance was modern, spotless and obviously well-considered.

At last they prepared to leave and Marisa offered Jack a lift in her car. He accepted, and said he would go back to the flat which he shared with a friend. His parents were wealthy; his mother, "a bit fussy". He had left the family home to look after himself.

At the brow of a hill, she braked and pulled in to the roadside when her mobile phone shrilly signaled a call. A wrong number. She switched the phone off. Night had fallen but the summer evening was not pitch dark and Marisa could tell Jack was watching her.

"Give *me* your number!"

She flushed, was glad of the protection of the darkness, and felt again that sense of uncertainty, the nagging worry about his age – and hers.

"Jack, I ..."

He did not speak for some moments and she found herself staring at his face, dimly visible. Her gaze lingering on the sensuous mouth. She was silent for moments, then sighed, frowned down at her phone, found "settings", and handed it to him.

He concentrated, added her number to his contacts, then shoved his own phone into a pocket.

When he looked up, he wore a quizzical air. He held the phone out to Marisa. His brow was furrowed with deep lines for such a young person. She reached out, and suddenly his arms went round her. The movement was unexpected and she gasped. Her face, buried his neck, was trapped for a moment with her lips against the warm skin of his collarbone.

They breathed quietly ... then, slowly and deliberately he tightened his hold, shifted to find her lips, and kissed her.

Passion leapt and Marisa, feeling helpless, responded.

* * *

Marisa's bungalow was located in a private lane, in a row of similar small, well-maintained properties where each had a large garden to the rear. If Piers was occasionally tempted to call her, he never took the liberty of visiting unexpectedly.

Before long, it was clear that, despite his youth, Jack liked to be in control. He was full of humour but he was assertive, and Marisa did not mind. She had become used to Piers' deferential manner. He offered ideas, but rarely argued the case for some shared activity in which she had no interest. Of course, without him, she was always in charge of her own plans. Being guided was something of an intriguing novelty.

Deeply into their relationship, Jack was intense. Much taller than Marisa, he had to stoop to kiss her, and would lift her face to meet his lips with his hand cupped beneath her chin. He brought gifts that must have reflected the way he saw her – rich dark chocolates, blood red roses and bottles of musk scented perfume. They were sumptuous, expensive, sophisticated treats. Summer evenings, she opened the front door and waited to hear Jack's quick footsteps as he crunched over gravel on the track in front of the houses. She saw him when he entered the driveway and crossed a paved area, to step into the hall with his arms outstretched to hold her at once.

Despite her relative maturity, Marisa was compliant in his arms, returning kisses but waiting until he was ready to take her into the bedroom, where he wrenched the clothes from her body. Their longing for one another was startling and thoughts of their age gap fled between the sheets. She tried to be pragmatic. "This is why some women deliberately look for a younger partner!"

In truth, she was astonished and thrilled by the way he was. She began to seem still more youthful; her skin acquired a translucent glow and her eyes sparkled. She let her curls grow, but tousled, and when she stood in her kitchen making their coffee Jack often found her wearing one of his sweatshirts over her slim, naked body. (It was a challenge; he was careful and possessive about his clothes and Marisa knew he would make her take it off!)

Sometimes, Jack arrived unexpectedly at the bungalow; it was always about making love but they talked too, and laughter aroused them both. As their eyes met, they would helplessly reach for each other.

* * *

Jack's parents were wealthy people, who loaded money into his account regularly. Marisa wondered if he minded.

"Do you wish they would leave you to manage on your own?" She hoped it wasn't a cheeky thing to ask. It was one of those moments, in conversation, when something sensitive is said a little thoughtlessly.

He wasn't offended. "Uh, well they want to make sure I'm okay ... it's cool," he said, in his easy way. He was not someone who had suffered for lack of money. "I'll look after them, some day."

For sure, a well-timed money gift was not a bad thing, Marisa agreed with him about that. She remembered how tough her university days were, when Charlie and Brenda did not understand that her student loan did not stretch very far.

Jack would find work for himself in any case, and since the end of his job in the local store he had already spent time in a coffee shop, taking over from a regular employee during a holiday.

A DREAM

Throughout the dreamlike summer, Jack was largely in control of their relationship. In early October the weather was colder some nights, and there came a spell of rain. Marisa still waited at the door, would open it when she saw him through the glass pane, and he still reached for her at once.

In the dimly lit hall, she stood barefoot on the burnt-orange carpet and it was warm in the house with a quietly humming central heating system. A few lamps glowed and there were scents of vanilla and Marisa's rich perfume.

She pinned herself to Jack's slender body, just as needy as she was at the start of their relationship.

* * *

A shared interest in music was a joy. Marisa, who had thought herself up-to-date, found Jack could introduce her to a wealth of new tracks from bands she had not known about before. She wondered if he had a beloved "old" band.

He didn't hesitate. "The Beatles!"

"Can't have them," she said decisively.

"Why not?" He wrapped his arms around Marisa, holding her fractionally too tight for comfort.

"Don't let me dow ... ow ... own ..."

52

She submitted to this indignity, but she argued. "Practically *everyone* loves the Beatles!"

"Hmm." He pondered this, and even told her she was weird, and "like a kid". She ignored the insults, waiting with her head against his chest. He finished the refrain from the Beatles. *"Nobody ever loved me like she does ... yeah, she does ... "* but then he offered Simply Red, and asked with exaggerated patience, did she like *them*?

"Yes! How could I not? That wonderful voice ...!" Marisa said.

Jack nodded, released her and went to recline on a sofa but his thoughts returned to the Beatles and he sang wistfully, *"... all about the girl who came to stay."*

Marisa rolled her eyes but she noticed he was watching her. "I didn't mean, I don't love the Beatles!" she said, argumentatively.

He upped the volume. *"When you say she's looking good, she acts as if it's understood – she's cool!"*

"Hey!" In a few steps she was behind his seat and had him around the neck with her forearm. It was easy for Jack to stop her throttling him and he reached up to tickle her ribs until she let him go.

"Get down here!" He dragged her from where she still leaned, and she slipped into the cushions with her head on his knees, where his tender embrace contradicted his rough words, as she knew it would. *"She's the kind of girl,"* he murmured *"... you want so much, it makes you sorry ..."*

* * *

They began to go out sometimes. Marisa tied her hair in a loose ponytail, wore a soft shirt with blue jeans or a neat short skirt and ballerina slippers. They made a personable couple and no one looked askance at them, but they avoided local venues, preferring to head for the bigger towns to find gigs, films or simply to wander together. They visited parks, ate in bistros or more sophisticated restaurants and were content.

When Jack began to talk about venturing further afield, Marisa suggested spending a few days in London. She urged him to let her choose a place to stay, and he agreed. In the hotel they were given a sumptuous room, equipped with all the essentials as well as treats and it was delicious to spend a few hours of the afternoon there, watching television, eating snacks from the refrigerator and raiding the mini bar. The gleaming bathroom was supplied with thick, white towels and sachets of rich bath oils and shampoo. Heavy curtains covered long windows in the living area, and carpets were opulent.

On the first evening, Marisa and Jack walked for a while before making their way to a restaurant. Again, the weather had altered, and now the air was warm with the very last of a summertime feel.

Marisa had secured her curls with a strip of yellow ribbon, thrown a white pashmina over her white suit, with its mini skirt and short sleeved jacket; and slipped her feet into strappy tan sandals.

Jack was dressed in a slim, collarless shirt, pale blue with tiny navy buttons. Over one shoulder was slung a cardigan, which he held with a forefinger hooked into the loop on the collar. He wore black skinny jeans and a pair of blue-and-white trainers. There were beaded and silver bracelets around his wrists.

"A hippy at heart?" Marisa teased. He denied that, and although he had let his hair grow longer in recent weeks, it was still trimmed into his preferred style with shorter sides. The crown was a mass of dark waves and with his wide mouth and brilliant eyes in a lean and handsome face, striding confidently on his long legs, he turned heads. He looked as if he might be a member of a rock band.

He was not unaware, Marisa knew. Skipping a few paces to keep up, she overheard a young woman make a frank comment to her companion. "I'd never get out of bed!"

Watching Jack, Marisa saw he remained impassive. Earlier, he said it was a special day. This was a comment which baffled Marisa, until he explained it was two months "since I dumped that awful job!" It was, therefore, two months since he held her hand for the first time. Before they left the hotel, he presented her with a silver charm – a tiny pendant, with a musical note imprinted on its surface.

They were in high spirits when, arm-in-arm, they entered their chosen restaurant. Once inside the door, where wall lamps glowed and a soft hum of conversation could be heard, a waiter came across the shining floor, to welcome them. Then, with a little shock of surprise, Marisa saw Piers standing at the bar.

The Restaurant

Piers wore a stunning dark suit. His gleaming white shirt was perfectly adorned with a narrow silver tie. When he turned around, his slender, polished black shoes squeaked faintly on the lacquered floor. His hair, greying just at the temples, was brushed smoothly back from his brow. Marisa and Jack joined him and the scent of his expensive cologne was in the air.

"Hey, Marisa!" His delight was obvious. She was thankful he did not say *my darling* but he gave her a kiss on the cheek. He glanced at Jack with a mannerly nod, before he asked how she was and offered her the tall stool he had been occupying. She declined and introduced the two men simply with the name of each one.

"This is Jack ..." Marisa placed slender fingers on Jack's sleeve. "Jack, this is Piers." They shook hands, briefly.

In lighthearted tones but carefully, she asked Piers only the most cordial and simple things. How was he? How was business? She made the short conversation easy, controlling it so that Jack would not feel discomfited by his lack of a connection with Piers, who bought their drinks before they moved away to their table. He picked up each glass and passed it to the recipient politely: Marisa, then Jack.

She saw him objectively, an almost impossibly smart man who, like herself, understood the etiquette of the situation. He wore a

watch but no jewellery; his hands were tanned, the fingernails man-
icured. The narrow streaks of grey at his temples only made him
look distinguished.

Jack took a swallow of his lager as they made their way to the
table. He chose a chair with its back to the bar. "He's a chief exec',
of something," she offered, vaguely.

"You don't want to tell me!" Jack's doubtful expression spoke
volumes. He went off to the toilets.

Marisa, seated, let her wrap slip from her shoulders. She looked
down into her glass, staring into the ruby red depths before she
drank most of the contents. She felt warm, and shed the little jacket
too, then turned and hung it over the back of her chair, and
scooped up the wrap, and made it into a neat roll, and placed it
behind her. She sat there in her thin top, with her arms bare, aware
of cool air being fanned over her skin by a nearby air conditioning
system. Nervously, she fingered the pearl and gold pendant around
her neck.

"Marisa," Piers' voice was gentle. At last she raised her head; saw
him standing just a few feet away. She met his eyes and saw he wore
an expression of kindness and good humour; and of course, he
would. "You look lovely!"

Certainly, he meant it, but Marisa was aware that, for an evening
with Piers she would have pinned up her hair, worn court shoes
(not sandals), and a light coat instead of a pashmina. She suited her
style to her man.

Piers was no fool. "How old is Jack?"

"He's alright ..." It was a childish non sequitur.

"No. How old? About twenty? *Marisa?*"

"Piers," she became defiant, stared back into the steady blue gaze.
"We're soul mates," she said.

A familiar dimple appeared by Piers' smiling mouth. He swirled
the brandy in his glass, waiting for seconds more with his free hand
in his pocket. Marisa did not volunteer anything further.

He finished his drink, sighed, removed his hand from the pocket of his jacket and stepped closer. He bent to kiss her brow, and at the same time he clasped her arm briefly. *"Take care of yourself,"* was all he murmured, but, straightening, he frowned, just a little, and regarded her for a fraction of a second more. Then with a barely perceptible nod, he turned, crossed the floor to leave the empty glass on the bar and headed towards the heavy *exit* doors. These were opened for him by a courteous waiter, who also held his coat, neatly folded over one arm. Piers was a regular customer. He accepted the coat, threw it around his shoulders, passed quickly through the open doorway and was gone.

Marisa probed her thoughts warily. She was used to Piers' tendency to seem lofty and did not mind it. Certainly, she had never identified it as the reason why she couldn't commit to him fully. He was adorable in many ways. This had been a significant incident, no matter how fast it happened; there was familiarity in Piers' words and his actions – how could things be otherwise? She mused over the gentle brush of his lips (no air kisses from Piers), and remembered he had grasped her upper arm quite firmly as he leaned down to her. The touch seemed to stay on her skin. She stroked the place with her palm, thinking it felt strange to receive her former lover's caress when she was deeply involved with Jack, no matter how casual the gesture seemed.

Did she feel foolish, because of the question about age? No! She was already glowing with the sense of being genuinely loved by Jack. Was she aware of some incongruity? She guessed so.

Marisa watched other diners for a few moments, aware of the soft hum of voices, seeing waiters crisscross the room without paying them any real attention. She let her thoughts wander, and confusion began to slip away. A chair was pulled from the opposite side of the table; Jack was there again, and she turned to him with a concern that leapt back into her heart. She prayed it was hidden. Was he calm?

He was smiling. "Hey!" She knew her face lit up, as she watched him settle into his place and reach for the menu.

They chose paella and, waiting, discussed a film, debating the worth of a review Marisa had read online. At last they finished their meal, and ordered coffee. Jack got up, and shifted his chair so he was beside her. Taking her hand, he kissed her fingertips and looked at her with his usual faintly cheeky expression. Tentatively, she asked, "Okay?"

He grinned. "Okay, Maris'!" All seemed well, and Marisa's sense of unease receded again.

Their coffee cups were empty, and Marisa and Jack prepared to leave. Marisa ate a mint fondant and Jack crammed two into his mouth before shrugging himself into his shawl collared cardigan. She stood up, checking the fastener on her clutch bag, and he took the little jacket and the white pashmina from the chair. He handled the garments carefully, and passed them over one at a time … but suddenly, hating herself, she had a rapid flow of thoughts. Jack liked nice clothes, and he had the grace to pick them up for her, and be careful, but Marisa couldn't help reflecting that Piers would have held the jacket open so she could shrug herself into it. He probably would even have wrapped her in the pashmina. She fought to dismiss such nonsense from her mind.

They returned to their hotel, walking hand-in-hand. Marisa had layered her clothes, but when a few spots of rain began to fall, she shivered and he pulled her against his side, drawing the heavy sweater around the two of them. She was wrapped and held closely, after all. She slipped her arm around his narrow waist, and tucked her thumb into his belt.

He kept her like that, unable to wriggle away as they entered the hotel foyer and managed, one-handed, to collect the keys to their room from the impassive clerk. He stuck the leather key fob between his teeth, and clamped a hand over her mouth when she tried to protest and they climbed a wide stairway with her crossly pulling at his fingers. He maintained a deadpan expression despite the keys dangling against his chin, and acknowledged the smiling interest of a passing maid with a nod. Another tricky manoeuvre and they entered their room in the same fashion, but there he whipped off the sweater, then Marisa's pashmina followed by her suit and her sandals, picked her up in his arms and took her straight to bed.

They were passionate as always, and held each other as they fell asleep. Feeling happy, Marisa put Piers out of her mind. She had split up with him after all – months before – and that was her own choice.

In the early hours of the next morning, she stirred and noticed they had left two low lights still burning. She leaned over from the bed to switch off the bedside lamp beside her, and then moved back, straightening the quilt. She glanced at the dim wall light and noticed, beneath its glow, Jack was lying with his eyes open.

"Okay?"

"Uh huh ..." It seemed he was. She assumed her movements had woken him, and thought little of it.

* * *

After a couple of days at home, Marisa received a call from Piers. He did not say, "Hello". Without preamble he asked, "Is he twenty? *Twenty?* He is – isn't he?"

"Nearly." Marisa thought she heard him mutter, *"Hell!"*

"But *I* love you!" he told her, before ringing off.

IF NOT ME?

Despite his apparent composure, following the events in London Jack revealed some sense of unhappiness. Marisa had set aside her worries with huge relief, and she could not believe what began to happen. Unexpectedly, he said he would go away – he thought, for a year. "To think".

"I don't want to leave you, but, I'm guessing, if it wasn't me, it would be Piers."

Sadly, she had to admit, she was with Piers for a long time. "But we broke up!" she insisted urgently, resisting the impulse to add *for goodness' sake!* She held on to his lapels, leaned her cheek against his chest. "It was my own choice, too!"

"I feel like that was only a *sort of* break-up?" Jack was very astute and now, with an awful shock for them both, he had spotted something she had been denying to herself, in a way.

Marisa felt desperate. She tried not to cry. "Jack! You must have seen other people before me! Surely you still respect them?"

He cupped her head with loving hands, but now he showed his youthful perception. "That's different," he said. "Girlfriends? Who cares? But I saw him Maris'. I just think ... well, maybe you would be best with someone ..."

She interrupted and it *was* a cry: "Oh Jack! I'm best with you!" They clung together. He must have let the sophistication of the

61

older man play on his mind and allowed himself to feel intimidated, but Marisa felt terribly hurt and thought, if the nameless girlfriends didn't matter, then neither should Piers.

A thought formed, but she couldn't voice it. "Remember how strong you were when those women were so rude?" Again, there was the possibility of a confrontation because of their differing ages. If she said something like that, she would surely seem patronising – even sly, if he felt beleaguered.

Of course, Marisa had no idea who Coco and the rest were. She had no visions of younger beauties to tease her emotions into jealous misery, whereas Piers had been right there in the bar with all his expensive style, his maturity and that undeniable familiarity. She remembered the kiss when they arrived at the bar, and thought regretfully that Jack may have witnessed the second kiss too, when Piers stooped down to say goodbye. Those were real kisses, not token gestures, and Marisa knew she had tried to brush them aside.

She could not put Jack under pressure to change. He disappeared for two days and although he answered her text messages briefly, confirming he was okay and he would see her soon – he volunteered nothing more.

"I'll go mad," Marisa thought unhappily. She wanted no-one but him.

At last he called, sounding excited and almost as soon as she said he could visit her, he appeared at her door, mobile phone in his hand. He wore a hat, a soft black fedora which he removed and slung on the floor as he bent to kiss her. It was not a gentle embrace, not at all. It felt like a signal – possessive, and confusingly, hungry as ever.

Marisa was afraid to question Jack but with a thudding heart she asked, was he staying?

He was, just for that one night. She would have been blissful but for the revelation that he was leaving the next day to travel to France and beyond. Marisa did not know how she prevented herself from begging to go too; she was devastated, knowing his excitement was because he had plans.

He had planned his route, worked out the costs, packed a bag. Marisa might have questioned this – one bag? Once again, she stopped herself from speaking naturally, feeling incredulous that, after all their closeness and the truly wonderful sense of being in tune with each other, now, she was so aware of her relative maturity!

The next morning, Jack stood before a mirror in the hallway, adjusting his collar with care, placing his hat *just so* on his cropped, dark hair. Marisa waited nearby. She had showered and pulled on a tee shirt and jogging bottoms, but she felt unsure of what to do. When she brushed her hair and sprayed perfume, forcing herself to at least try to be memorable, she wondered if it was worth it. Would Jack remember her fondly? Was he actually slipping away for good? It was a situation that some women would have treated very differently. Should she have shown her distress? Why not be furious? She could tell Jack he was hurting her so much, if he really went away now, he was never to return!

He was oddly methodical in his preparations. It was as if there was no drama in his actions; decision made, he would go ahead regardless of the disbelief and pain playing out in Marisa's mind, and with this behaviour he made it impossible for her to scream. What if she did, and he didn't care? What if she did, and he smiled? Could she tell him she loved him? Spontaneity was lost in any case, and Marisa was weighing up her every action; but she hadn't said those words before, and at this moment, sadly, they might sound desperate.

She *was* seesawing emotionally, and yet Marisa knew that she would always want him back. If she was to save any hope of it, she must conduct her farewell very carefully. Still, the sorrow was deep and a question escaped. "Oh Jack! What is this all about, really?"

He turned at once, to hold her. In his arms, Marisa struggled not to act like a tearful teenager. She tried to stand up straight. He lowered his face to hers, looking from beneath the brim of the hat into her eyes with his usual brilliance, making her stomach turn over with the thrill he always gave her.

But Jack was full of barely suppressed excitement; she felt his tension when he kissed her and she wondered if he did not fully understand what their separation would be like. He was not being fair, but Marisa was wise enough to understand that – in his own mind – he did not think he was doing the wrong thing.

He kissed her, then he turned her to face a row of cinema and gig tickets, pinned up on a board, along with a champagne cork suspended by string. "All those times!"

She sighed and turned back. He clasped her sorrowful face between warm palms. "Maris', it'll be okay."

* * *

Inevitably, Marisa hated feeling abandoned. Still, she would not date casually, just to stop herself from being alone. In a quandary, she set aside her work for a week or two, and went to visit her parents, where she stayed for a few days before moving on. She did not confide in them, and typically they enjoyed her company for a long weekend and let her go without questioning her, as soon as she was ready. She would spend some time by the sea.

Deliberately seeking comfort, feeling physically weakened by her emotional pain, Marisa chose a hotel, so that she did not have to make her own meals or maintain the rooms she inhabited on her own for several days. It was strange to wake up each morning and find herself lying in the centre of an unfamiliar bed, but comforting when she heard the rattle of china and the murmur of voices, on her way down the wide staircase, to breakfast.

She knew no-one, involved herself with no friendly stranger just for the sake of a little conversation, and walked for miles along the sea front. Sometimes she stopped, and sat on a bench to stare out across the ocean. Wrapped in a thick white fleece jacket and a wide brown woollen scarf, her hands in a pair of fur gloves, she gazed and dreamed, and her silky curls were whisked across her face by the wind.

The cry of gulls was a tolerable sound on a happy day by the sea, thought Marisa. It seemed mournful because of her sorrow, and the surging grey waves were a chilly, backdrop to the scene on the beach. A few walkers made their way along the sands with their dogs, pointlessly throwing sticks or pebbles for animals that were running around and exercising anyway.

Marisa was not in touch with Jack now. She could not change anything. Possibly he *would* return – he had made a promise after all – but he was young and ardent, and he would find new adventures on his travels.

She thought about the way she let Jack go. They shared her bed on that last night, even though she knew he would leave without her. She tried not to make a big fuss the next day. Marisa did not regret her behaviour, for it was a choice. With a supreme effort, she had conducted herself in a way that she thought might bring him back, feeling confident of her love, her lack of censure, and her patience.

Months before, when he began to walk away in the park, she had let her heart rule her head. She ran after him. This time, although she had shown her love once again, she would not try to chase him. He was terribly sensitive. Perhaps he was selfish but, with compassion, Marisa knew Piers had presented a real challenge to the pride of the younger man.

Definitely, Piers would remain adoring. For her part, with this shocking turn of events have forced her to face the truth, Marisa knew she loved them both.

Would it be wise to marry Piers, in a life choice made consciously, in her own best interests? Wise, perhaps … but no, Marisa still thought she would not marry Piers.

Should she reject Jack, if he wanted her again? The idea did not feel like wisdom, but madness! It seemed, if Jack failed to return, she might be lonely forever.

THE LONG YEAR

Marisa was so sad, and so conflicted when she contemplated her long wait for Jack, she felt oddly distanced from reality. She had no intention of rushing to tell Piers what had happened but he was in the habit of calling on the telephone occasionally, and when he took it into his head to catch up with her, he noticed a change in her voice.

"You aren't well," he said, in one of his unarguable observations. Unable to stop herself, Marisa told him she was alone and the admission provoked her tears. He immediately wanted to be with her.

Marisa could not pretend she thought Piers would keep away, after that. "I'm on my way," he told her. "I'll ..." There was a pause. "It's four o'clock. Look, I can leave here in twenty minutes, and grab a bag from my flat, and I should reach you by around six thirty!" It wasn't a question, nor a mere suggestion. He *was* on his way.

She nodded even though she could not be seen, then found her voice. "Thank you."

Waiting for Piers, Marisa knew she should be full of mental turmoil. He would want to be everything to her, all that he could be, and he was a powerful force. How could she welcome this former lover, this dear friend, when she missed Jack so badly? When the break-up was so recent? She was very tired, and trying to face herself with the rights and wrongs of her behaviour felt like an impossible challenge. Suddenly, she knew she wouldn't do it. She turned away from the hall telephone, went into the bathroom and filled the bathtub with hot, foamy water.

When, at last, Marisa saw Piers' silhouette through the glass panels of her front door, she went along the hallway, let him in, wept again and was weakly swept into his strong embrace.

* * *

Piers wore a sweatshirt and jeans, and his forelock of thick hair, usually so smoothly brushed, fell into his eyes. He hugged Marisa tightly, then lifted her and headed for the kitchen. Set apart from the mismatched seats and the table, there was a deep, cushioned, basket chair. He stowed her into it, and disappeared for a few seconds, then returned with a throw which he'd found at the foot of her bed. She stopped crying and submitted to being warmly covered, and watched in silence as he moved confidently about the room, opening a coffee jar, boiling water, spooning sugar and at length bringing hot coffee in her favourite porcelain mug.

Marisa was in pain, but she knew Piers well, and she wasn't blinkered to the fact that he was distraught. It crossed her mind that he felt guilty, since he was used to supporting her, even from the distance she made him keep. When he met Jack, he must have feared her happiness would be short-lived, and events seemed to have shown he was right. She sipped her coffee and was again aware of deliberately letting her mind slide away from the conflict within. She would face her conscience … well … some time.

Meanwhile, Piers was not about to face her with anything at all. Calmly, he picked up a steaming cup of coffee for himself. He drew up a chair, and sat near Marisa, watching her with a weary expression in his eyes. He remained silent.

* * *

When Marisa awoke the next morning, she found Piers lying by her side, patiently waiting for her to open her eyes and know she was not alone. He had wrapped his large frame in a towelling robe, which he must have brought with him. His cologne scented the air, and she guessed he had been awake for some time – showering, perhaps. Worrying, for sure. Letting her sleep on.

Restlessly, she moved as if to leave the bed, but he reached for her, and closed his fingers around her shoulder.

"Marisa!" He spoke gently.

"He's not a saint!" The words formed in her mind, but in the same moment, she sank into his arms.

* * *

By December, Marisa was spending much of her time with Piers. Never a dull companion, full of conversation and plans, he was so very kind and the temptation to be in his arms, to allow him to comfort and support her hurt self, was overwhelming. Marisa believed Jack had gone, if not for good, certainly for the year he proposed.

So, she was cushioned from the classic state of awful desperation of the abandoned partner – and yet, it was only a partial protection. In her heart, Marisa was in torment, for everywhere she saw Jack lookalikes and she could not forget him.

No one had his presence. The most handsome young man could cross her path, and she felt a jolt of recognition for barely a second, then a renewed agony of loneliness. It was desperately hard simply to stop herself from crying. She could not eat properly, and began to lose weight from her stomach and thighs, where she had been perfect. She observed herself objectively, feeling detached in a way because – without Jack there to admire her – she did not care. Cinching in her belts, she decided her clothes looked pretty good, but her face looked wan.

The process of regaining a sort of normality was slow, and she faltered often. Inevitably, guilty feelings crowded in and some of them were for Piers and his own safety and peace of mind. Just once, Marisa raised her voice, to cry, *"You shouldn't stay with me!"* Still, she never told him, *"You should go!"*

At the age of forty-one, Piers was a desirable man. He looked after himself, played squash, went regularly to a gym, and swam in deliberate efforts to keep himself in peak fitness. Marisa had no idea about other women in his life, and knew it was unlikely there were none; however, he was clearly determined to stay with her for as long as she wanted his company. She never saw any of the telltale signs of significant, different relationships in his life; his mobile phone wasn't hidden, ever, and he spent every minute – when he wasn't working – either by her side, or in contact. Respectfully, she didn't chase him if he went off to the sports hall, and when he was late after work sometimes, she assumed it was unavoidable, believing it was not for her to question him.

Piers' interest in music was mainly slanted towards the classical but although Marisa was perfectly happy to go to a concert with him, or listen to some ethereal piece he loved, she liked modern music. She acknowledged that older bands were valuable but thought that where there were new tracks constantly being created, she preferred to keep up. It was where she had common ground with Jack; their shared love of gigs was more rewarding for Marisa.

Piers behaved almost exactly as he always had, but something was happening, and he began to tune in to different radio stations.

"What's this?" He hummed a tune.

"Two Door Cinema Club," she told him. "*What You Know.* It's nice."

"I listened to it!" he said. "The lyric goes ... *I can tell just what you want. You don't want to be alone.* It reminds me of you, Marisa." He did not add (but Marisa knew) a line in the song went, *it's my sweet beginning.*

His efforts to be modern were a bit behind, she thought. Had she fallen into a tender little trap? Another line was, *you've known it the whole time. Yeah, you've known it ...*

Piers was trying hard and his efforts made her heart ache, as she noticed, increasingly, his wish to seem youthful. It was surely a conscious effort. He took her rowing, wore casual clothes and teased her. Lacking strength, she could not make much headway when she took a turn on the oars. There was a poignancy in their fun, for he spoilt nothing and his efforts to be lighthearted worked, were a diversion, made her laugh and relax.

They spent a long weekend in France, where they made a rule for themselves and tried to speak no English for three whole days. Language was not a problem for either one, but *"Je t'aime"* Piers told Marisa and she could not say it back.

* * *

Upon their return from France, Piers addressed their shared dilemma directly, although he made sure he spoke about Marisa's situation with the most emphasis.

"You are too pretty, too vibrant and clever, *far too young,* to stay in and just wait," he said. "There are places to see, people to talk to! Come with me, we've got time. We'll travel, for a while."

He had money but so did Marisa, and it was not embarrassing to be offered treats. She agreed to travel and considered they both had their eyes wide open to the complexities of their involvement. Was this odd, even very wrong? The possibility of Jack's return was there, and the knowledge that Marisa waited was a burden for both herself and Piers.

On a cruise, a whole month at sea in wonderful luxury, she enjoyed all the sights and experiences of the trip across the Mediterranean. Piers was relentless in his attention to Marisa's comfort and happiness, but he liked to be active and when she would have lain helplessly on her bed or the sundeck, he teased gently until she agreed to join in. They played squash or badminton, and swam in the great pool on the ship, and the activity sometimes made Marisa abandon her cares for a while. Both she and Piers could laugh, especially when there were other travellers around to share their sport.

Inevitably, her sorrow returned, and perhaps also inevitably, there came a moment when she saw Piers, too, was quite sad.

Foolishly, believing he was sleeping where he lay on a recliner with his eyes closed, she allowed her gaze to follow the progress of a dark-haired young man as he jogged past them along the deck. Recalling a conversation about birthday months and birth signs, she reflected Jack must be twenty, now. In itself, the thought didn't affect her very much, since it made no difference to her feelings. When she glanced back at Piers, she was not making any kind of comparison, letting her mind wander, idly wondering if he had woken. He was watching her. He said nothing but at the dinner table he did not engage in conversation with their companions. He ordered whisky to be brought in a jug, poured it over ice and, later, added it to his coffee too.

In the cabin, where they shared a neat space and a comfortable bed, Piers was quiet but not hostile. He made fresh coffee and brought her cup to the bedside, where he placed it on a tiny fold-out shelf. Marisa had given up trying to read a magazine; she set it aside and leaned forward to wrap her arms around his neck. In a little while, they made love and instead of peacefully falling asleep, he lay with his head on her breast for a long time. She stroked his brow, musing in the lamplight, fingering the heavy, grey-streaked lock of dark hair that fell into his eyes when he relaxed. She knew that Piers would always try to withhold blame, because he really loved her.

"I heard another song," he murmured.

"Piers!"

He ignored her. "Mumford & Sons ... *The Cave.*"

"Mm, well I do know it." She tried to be humorous, and slipped up again. "It's sort of sweet, but it's a bit of a dirge!"

"A dirge," he repeated reflectively."

I will hold on hope and I won't let you choke
On the noose around your neck ....

There would be no dirge for Marisa because he would not let her die of pain over Jack, but Piers offered no argument. After all, was the knell sounding for his relationship with her, no matter how hard he tried to chase away the gloom? Of course, it was. He was supporting, even saving her, but he faced losing her, and lamenting, one day.

* * *

There was no doubt in Marisa's mind that she loved Piers. She trusted and admired him, times with him were good and happy, inasmuch as she could be content. He would love her always and offer her security, but Marisa knew she had two loves. She thought she understood why some people are unfaithful in a marriage. Not the serial cheats who seek cheap thrills, pretending to be single and looking for extra-marital affairs. The lovers.

Would she be able to refuse Jack if he returned? No. Whatever might happen, she would never send Jack away.

Still, then, she would not marry Piers. They faced each other on board the ship where they stood together at the rail as the journey ended. Choking on guilty words, she confessed, "I can't commit!"

Piers lost his composure. He looked down, then back at Marisa's face. "What *is it* about him?" he asked, painfully.

A breeze whipped strands of silky hair across Marisa's face. She hated Piers' question. He was not trying to ridicule her, and she could guess his reference to Jack was the last thing he meant to say, but he showed naked emotion, confusion and, perhaps, all the feelings he had been struggling to cope with. He had made her feel callous, and she closed her eyes against the pain she saw in his face and tried to bear the suffering in her own heart.

"Piers, don't! Don't do that ... don't ..." Her breath was gone, lost on the sea breeze and a tide of emotion.

* * *

Piers refused to leave Marisa. He said simply, he would wait. Perhaps he was just *holding on to hope*, but he did not challenge her again. He had pulled himself together.

After the long holiday, they both began to live at the bungalow. It was a comfortable arrangement and they fell into a routine, just as they had a few years before. She worked in her study; he drove to London most weekdays and in the evenings, they shared a meal. Sometimes they would take a stroll to the local pub or, if the day had been warm, they reclined in the hot tub situated in the garden underneath the sitting room window. They drank white wine or sparkling water, and chatted. It should have been so peaceful and nice ... it *was* a bit like being married.

The situation was not unusual, in a way. Many sorrowing lovers turn to a new companion. Bereft and hurt, Marisa was lucky to have someone to comfort her. In bizarre complexity however, Piers suspected that upon Jack's return she would want only Jack; Marisa, who could not hope to conceal her longing, was unable to contradict him; and yet, still, he tried his hardest to win her heart for himself.

On Sunday mornings, Piers liked to drink sherry, relaxing while he read the papers. He dressed casually, with his shirt-sleeves rolled up, wearing shorts or light trousers and a pair of much cherished, dreadfully battered old sandals. He sat in a garden chair near the fishpond on the last Sunday of August. A gentle breeze lifted the corners of the newspaper and ruffled his hair. Disarmed, Marisa stooped and kissed him on the cheek in passing as she brought her own glass to the iron filigree table where he had placed his sherry bottle.

He looked up. "Do you love me more, now?" It was a question

which was uncharacteristic, and Piers generally chose not to be so forthright. However, they had travelled for over eight weeks and lived together in her bungalow for a further month. The history they shared before that could never be denied.

"More?" She affected a careless tone, poured her drink and turned away. She picked up a miniature watering can with a long spout, and began to freshen up some plants. More than before? More than she loved Jack? Please let it be the first one, thought Marisa.

"… than you did?" He frowned at a page, avoiding her eyes to guard his feelings a little from her response.

More than before then, thank goodness. "I do love you, Piers, you know that."

It was no accident that this exchange was made without facing one another. They were living in a perpetual state of distress, beneath the civil and sensible, even loving surface. Piers was waiting for Marisa to change her mind, but she was waiting for Jack, and after almost twelve months, the silence hurt worse than ever.

Piers read on, while Marisa drank more sherry than she usually allowed herself. With her emotions somewhat blunted, she played housewife and created a classic roast meal, with crisp parsnips and creamed swede to accompany chicken and roasted potatoes, because those were some of his favourite foods. After they shared red wine while they ate, Marisa and Piers decided against dessert and then, bearing a coffee tray and quite pleasantly and disgracefully drunk, they went to bed.

* * *

That evening, with no one to tell of her deepest thoughts, Marisa whispered to her koi as she knelt to scatter their food. "Piers is adorable," she confessed. She placed the bag beside her, bending closer to the surface of the water where the great fish gleamed red, white, black-spotted and golden. She shed a few tears, dashed them away with the back of her hand and bit her lip. "He is, but I hurt, without Jack. If he doesn't come home when the year is up, I will still be waiting. If he does ... well ... oh dear!"

She bent her head, and saw the way her thin print skirt lay across her lap, and looked at her hands with clasped fingers, resting on her knees. A memory came unbidden to her thoughts, of the way Jack had tightly held both her hands when they sat together, in the park.

When she stood up at last, she glanced towards the house and saw that Piers was there, motionless in the bay window, watching her with a serious expression.

* * *

At the end of the month, Piers was forced to go to stay in London. He had meetings scheduled in his diary, and his days would be so busy; it would not be practical to drive back and forth, night and morning.

"Join me?" he asked. "At least, for a few days? We can stay somewhere nice. You'll shop; we'll share lunches, and evenings at the theatre ... or just walking around London!" He was trying to tempt her. "If you prefer, you could have a proper rest again, and we could simply spend our evenings quietly, eat in the hotel and talk!"

She knew it would be an enjoyable week, if she agreed to go with him. They were never short of conversation, and they usually missed out the part where Marisa waited for Jack.

She wouldn't go. Saddened because he knew the reason, he was calm nevertheless. "It's a year, isn't it?"

"Yes."

In the morning, Marisa awoke to find the space beside her in the bed was cool and empty. Afraid that Piers had left, she leapt up. To her relief, she found him in the bathroom, where he was placidly shaving, humming quietly as he squinted into the mirror.

He saw her reflection when she appeared beside him, and cast her a sidelong glance. "Marisa!" She had grabbed a scarf, but it hardly covered her modesty. She could not say he had scared her, could not raise his hopes, although, when he cast the razor down and turned to hold her, she understood, would not reject him, and entered his embrace.

There were gifts beside her cereal bowl. Marisa, dressed in a shirt and a pair of soft trousers, slid into her chair, tipped muesli into the dish and reached for a jug of milk. She eyed the small heap of treats and turned her head to smile as Piers entered the kitchen. He looked smart, groomed and composed.

"These are lovely things!" she said. "Thank you!"

He had given her a compact disc, a box of luxurious Belgian chocolates and a delicate platinum charm. Strung on a chain, it was in the shape of a fish. The music was by the Kooks, and he played a track before he left: *I always thought I would end up with you, eventually ...*

"Oh, Piers!" Marisa couldn't finish her breakfast. They hugged, in a lingering embrace.

Piers would return to his private flat in London. He was taking suitcases packed with all his clothes, but she would not allow herself to be upset over this strong sign of pessimism over their shared future. It was her fault, after all.

He kissed her. "Take care." He was warm and familiar. Marisa knew, too, that he was very brave. Leaving her there was a risk that affected his own happiness.

Later that day, he contacted her, wanting to say just one more thing as he often did after leaving her alone. "Marisa ... dearest Missy," he said. "He may not return."

"I know." Awkwardly, she replied. "I do know ... but also, he might."

In a way, Piers had given her mixed messages but Marisa understood them. He called her with loving intent, and that lyric – "thought I would end up with you *eventually*" – spoke volumes. He hoped, and he could not alter his feelings, and would not hide them. However, he knew only too well, there was no easy decision for Marisa just yet. All his possessions were gone from the bungalow and he was set to stay away.

"Not *mixed* at all then," she thought, beginning to drive herself a bit crazy as lovers do. "It's clear. He loves me but he will wait and see what I ... what ... happens."

Would Piers see other women in London? He was very attractive, rich and generous. If the opportunity arose for Marisa to choose between the two men she loved and (of course) *if she chose Jack,* Piers was not a man who would want to remain single. She did not really expect him to wait until she made her decision, although she suspected he would. She entertained the thought of his possible interests elsewhere for just a moment and found it bearable, as long as she did not dwell.

It was a different matter when she pondered that Jack – young, vibrant and loving – probably spent time with women during the long year. The emotional pain was immediately so great, Marisa wondered if it was possible to die of it. Not *"probably,"* she told herself. *"Definitely."* She had to physically drag herself out of her chair, get out of the house and try to stop thinking about it.

September

Marisa felt aimless, and she could not tolerate sitting at her computer. She was unable to concentrate on her work, or care about a normal routine. Dully, she turned out a few kitchen cupboards. Her mind was not on the task but, slowly, she began to tidy and clean more of her surroundings. Desultory at first, then enthusiastic as she created a pleasant environment, she found new energy, and some comfort in mindless activities. She vacuumed and dusted the sitting-room, and the hallway. She polished a mirror, remembering the small mementos that once were saved on a corkboard beneath the stair rail. They were still cherished, but they had been put away in a drawer a long time ago.

When Marisa turned her attention to the bedroom, she changed all the linen and shifted furniture around. At the windows, she hung a heavy pair of new velvet drapes. Floor-length; deep blue in colour; they had been set aside during the summer months.

Feeling dissatisfied with the contents of her cupboards, she went hastily to the corner shop where the interior had been refitted and there was a complete change of staff. For months, Marisa had avoided the shop and it wasn't difficult with Piers around. They had eaten out in restaurants; ordered meals which were delivered to the bungalow; shopped online, and called one another sometimes during the day to arrange for Piers to collect items on his way home.

At last, it appeared the local shop employed properly trained staff, and a smart young woman looked at her directly and asked if she needed any help! Once her transaction was complete, the assistant hoped she would have a nice day.

With a collection of cleaning products weighing down her bags, Marisa returned home. She energetically scrubbed the bathroom until, scented strongly with lemon instead of lingering reminders of men's aftershave and shower gels, the smart white units shone and the black and white tiled floor gleamed. A posy of pansies in a fluted glass stood on the white tiles of the narrow sill, along with a row of pink and yellow bottles of air fragrances; fresh soap was placed by the sink, and at last the room had an entirely feminine ambiance.

In the longer term, she knew she disliked a solitary life. The child she once was, left alone in her room where she studied so hard, needed an occasional kindly visit from a mother with a cup of tea in her hand, a feeling of pride in her heart, an expression of encouragement, but Marisa's lazy parents never saw it and thus a form of neglect caused some harm.

For the time being, she did not feel lonely, and somehow her sensitivities were stilled. When she tired of housekeeping activities, instead, she became aimless and, matching behaviour to emotions, spent much of her time in daydreams. If she wanted to unburden herself of deep thoughts, she told the koi, and afterwards let her emotions return to a kind of equilibrium. When she needed to cuddle something warm, there was the neighbour's affectionate cat. For someone who would share an inconsequential chat, there was Derek, the gardener who came to work each afternoon, just for an hour or two.

She dragged an armchair to a new position so that, curled up with a novel to read, she had a view from her window into the peaceful garden, where Derek stooped over his tasks. He picked up the last of the fallen apples, tied long stemmed plants to stakes, and dead-headed flowers, and his preparations for autumn were nicely in tune with Marisa's efforts indoors.

Marisa always met Derek with a cup of tea when he arrived, but later, musing and daydreaming, she remained in her chair. When he was ready again for a drink, sometimes he would lift his hand in a tipping motion, miming drinking, whereupon she gave him a thumbs-up sign. It was a small, shared joke. *Might she make tea? No, go ahead, he could do it* ... and then he would nod, point to indicate his direction, and leave his work to potter into her kitchen and switch on a kettle to brew tea for them both.

Derek had liked Jack well enough and commented sparely, that he had an old soul, for a youngster. He got along better with Piers, who would discuss gardening projects with grave interest. For Marisa, Derek had a straightforward point of view about Piers too: quite simply, he thought Piers should stay. She did not share her own thoughts but she listened, did not express how painful it was to be confronted with Jack's youth, or Piers' suitability, and respected the elderly man and whatever wisdom he wished to impart.

Marisa's interests during her years of study and in her work focused upon the English language, history of English and the perfection of the written word. She did not consider herself to be deeply analytical but, with time on her hands, she became reflective and dwelt on the ways in which Derek compared with her father. Obviously, the gardening ... and this consideration inevitably led her to spot the differences. Charlie never brought tea for her, nor would he have offered thoughts about her life and plans. Years on from the effects of that reserved disinterest, she could try to take a philosophical view.

To receive her secrets, she chose her fish. Impassively goggling, silently swimming, they knew nothing except their watery environment and occasionally the appearance of their food when it appeared on the surface of the pond. So, because she had a plan that defied convention, Marisa murmured, sometimes, to the oblivious creatures. They couldn't argue, and giving voice to her thoughts helped Marisa to work through them. In this way, she recognised her fundamental belief that Jack would return. She would not be thwarted.

Nevertheless, in a moment of uncertainty, Marisa bent forward with her head in her hands. She was seated in her chair near the window. Before long, Derek was there, bearing – not tea – but a shot of whisky. To collect the drink for her, he must have gone back to his own house a few doors away, since she did not keep a whisky bottle when Piers was absent. Derek was in stockinged feet, being careful, as usual, not to leave muddy footprints indoors.

She accepted the drink and the kind gesture with a smile. He stood beside her for a few moments, resting a weather-beaten hand on the back of her chair, before quoting a phrase: *When I was a child, I spake as a child, I understood as a child, I thought as a child: but when I became a man, I put away childish things.* It was a biblical reference. "One Corinthians," he added. "King James Bible."

Delivered of this impossibly obtuse comment, Derek returned to his plants.

* * *

Days passed. Marisa listened to music, ate simply, indulged in leisurely bubble baths and lingered over a meticulous manicure. She took care of herself, but making a hairdresser's appointment felt like a pointless waste of time, so her pale gold-brown curls grew long, and her hair generally lay in an untidy knot on the nape of her neck.

Was Piers hoping, even believing, she would make the most sensible choice, and, of course, that it would be him? Did he trust her to understand he was the better man, and was that at the root of his immense courage? He would allow himself to be persuaded of a future together, if she told him she no longer waited for Jack. If she wanted to save herself from being alone, then the option was there, but Marisa was not cold-hearted and she respected Piers. Besides, she still waited, since the long year was yet to draw to its full conclusion.

Marisa never disclosed her passion for Jack to Julia, and keeping it secret was not difficult because of their distance apart. Julia was building her new life, coaching her clients, and it was easy for Marisa to say she was busy if the subject of arranging a meeting arose. They had maintained a certain friendship despite differing lifestyles, and there was fun and laughter when they spent time together, but they had not met for many months. Marisa made her own decisions and sharing her innermost thoughts about relationships was not a natural thing for her to do.

When Piers left again, Marisa had no wish to be urged to change her mind and she did not confide in Julia. There was no need at all to explain that the person who consumed her emotions and for whom she waited, was a friend of Julia's student son.

* * *

The early weeks of September went by. "I'm alright, in a way!" Marisa reflected, taking some comfort from Piers' continued civilised behaviour. She felt lucky to be free to make choices, even though his kind efforts to bring her around to his way of thinking had tugged at her heartstrings. Again, she returned to those sensitive, linked truths, which never seemed to let her stamp them out. "It *is* quite possible that Jack will never show up here again. I could marry Piers, and he would be a dear, and he would love me."

She also considered that, if she was entirely objective, it was conceivable she could travel anywhere in the world and find some nice man who would love her just as much as Piers did, offering a fresh start. New experiences could be found, yet why would any woman hunt for a different Piers? He was practically perfect, someone to fight for and who so clearly fought for her, in his own way. He was doing the best he could, and letting her be alone now was part of the plan. It was fair enough.

She turned her attention more closely to the question of whether or not to she should widen her opportunities. "I am a whole person," she insisted. "I am not just an attachment to a man!"

Inevitably, she wondered: if her horizons were forced to open up, was there any likelihood that she would meet *another Jack?* It was hopeless, her train of thought seemed to grab the phrase *open up* as if she had little control over her own mind. Startled, Marisa suspected no one would ever compare to him. She took her laptop from its case, lifted the lid, searched for definitions of existentialism and puzzled over them, deliberately trying to move her perceptions to a new plain.

At last, equipped with knowledge but having changed nothing, Marisa poured Chardonnay into a great glass of the sort the health police warn against, went into her garden, and found herself walking slowly in circles, on the springy, freshly-mown lawn.

She understood *existentialism,* a philosophy where one seeks to find oneself living peacefully in the moment. It seemed to mean being satisfied – not looking back and not hungering for what the future may hold. It was interesting to reflect that her parents had always lived that way. Interesting and somewhat depressing, thought Marisa. What about hope, and passion, and ambition?

"I should probably talk about it with Derek!" she thought. "I can't, though. He would spot what I'm up to, and I want to sort it out for myself!"

After all, the answers for Marisa were not really elusive and she arrived at them in her own way. "I don't need to think about who I am or what my life is all about, when Jack is here … I'm content … even blissful! So, Jack and I can just exist, in the moment *together,* with ambition shelved but passion hardly ever spent!

"For Piers and I … there is love. There is, for sure." She remembered a line from one of the songs he liked: *… and I will change my ways.* She sighed. "I just don't think it's enough. When it is Piers,

I'm still seeking more."

* * *

Jack had never told Marisa he loved her. *If he returned would it be love that brought him back?* Did that even matter to Marisa, just as long as he did come home? Would she have him back at any cost?

Considering his youth and all the opportunities he must have – so handsome and personable – eventually she decided that, loving Jack as she did, she would wait. If he appeared again, she would consider herself lucky! She would try to be everything he wanted. Feminists would consider her plan too self-effacing, but Marisa knew any different perspective was doomed to failure.

"This is it! It's just the way I am. My heart leads." It was a romantic choice; potentially, a painful one.

At the end of the final week in September, after taking a brief call from Piers in which he was matter-of-fact and somewhat hurried (just checking in before a meeting perhaps?) Marisa wandered along her hallway when she heard the snap of her letterbox. Letters were landing on top of a couple of things; she collected them in a handful and found a plastic-wrapped slip of a parcel. A free gift? She hoped it was not pet treats but no, it contained muesli. Still holding the sachet along with the post, she bent and picked up a new compact disc which also lay on the mat. Not hidden by a wrapper, it was Simply Red's *Stars*. Her heart began to pound.

Marisa played the music at once, getting goosebumps, knowing it could not have been Piers who delivered it.

I wanna fall from the stars, straight into your arms ...

A tall glass full of white tulips stood in the exact centre of her kitchen table. She propped her muesli packet against it and placed the cd case there too. All day she pondered over the lyrics.

You'll never know how much you hurt me ...

She played the track again and again.

A Different
Kind of Cool

Evening came. Barefoot, Marisa wandered along the soft carpet of her hallway and out through the front door, where she picked an armful of perfect, fluffy dahlias from the border under bay windows, snapping stems, knowing Derek would tell her to get the secateurs.

Bathed in the last of the evening sunshine, with her hands full of glowing flowers, Marisa was tanned to golden and the skin on her shoulders, breast and cheekbones was supple and gleaming. Her abundant, caramel-coloured hair, shot with blonde lights, was drawn into a loose knot. She wore a white cotton dress, belted at the waist with a narrow strip of fawn leather.

She saw a movement behind the hedge beyond her lawn, saw there was someone arriving on foot and he stopped at her gateway.

Slim legs in jeans and dusty boots; a colorful wrap ... *long dark locks of wavy hair*, a beard.

She closed her eyes, covered them with both hands, heard quick footsteps over the gravel then she was being pulled up and enfolded in his arms.

"Jesus! Marisa, you still do that? *Open your eyes!*"

Overwhelmed with relief, hearing his familiar lazy voice like the balm she'd so longed for, she buried her face in the folds of the red and orange cape that was slung around Jack's shoulders. Breathed in mixed scents of musk cologne and marijuana. Grasped a handful of rough material and asked, "Cannabis?"

"It's okay in Amsterdam!"

"You were in Amsterdam?" She didn't really care about the scent of marijuana, or where Jack was before this moment.

"Last month. I'll tell you where I went, later." Jack kissed her.

He was pulling at her belt, quite hard, drawing her hips towards him, then he slid his hand with the palm against her body, slowly all the way back up to her face, lifted her chin with firm fingers, just shades away from being too rough. Her legs were folding, as he kissed her again then swiftly released the silver buckle at her waist, lifted her into his arms and carried her through the open doorway to her bed.

In the white-and-cream painted bedroom, the heavy velvet drapes were not quite drawn together but the evening was darkening outside and the light was dim. A sash window was open, and a gentle breeze slipped between the drapes, and cooled the air around Marisa and Jack, where they held one another in a passionate and loving embrace, behind the wafting nets around her bed.

* * *

Jack lit a cigarette, leaning back against pillows, lowering dark lashes as he relaxed. An owl could be heard intermittently hooting, from a perch in the trees at the foot of the garden.

Marisa sat up and scooped her loosened curls into a topknot, watching Jack's face. He was deeply tanned but looked drawn and tired, although he had lost an air of tension. He drew his fingers across his eyes in a weary gesture. Idly, or so it seemed, he posed a question. "Did you know I would come back?" He wasn't looking at Marisa.

"No," she answered. "I hoped. I didn't *know* ..." Unsaid, were the words "*... and I was so afraid*".

She felt her mouth going dry, for here he was but somewhat

altered, and she dreaded what might come next. Was he going to tell her he would take off again? Marisa tried to keep her cool. She studied her fingernails and tried to affect similar unconcern. "Did you know I would wait?" she asked.

He smiled, glanced at her, then tapped ash from the cigarette into the empty packet beside him. With the other hand, he reached for her chin, turned her face towards his and briefly tugged a curl that fell over her forehead. "Yeah," he said in his laconic way. "I reckon I knew." He frowned then again stared into space. "Near the end of the year, I hoped I was right."

Jack smoked again then stubbed out his cigarette and exhaled. He turned on his side to draw her close. He rested his chin on her head and stroked her shoulders very gently, smoothing the sun-tanned skin, tickling the nape of her neck, breathing quietly, seeming reflective.

Marisa's fingertips were light on his chest. He felt stronger, broader than before. It crossed her mind fleetingly that Derek's convoluted comment was essentially a prediction and it had come true. Jack was a man, now.

After a few moments, he spoke again. Tenderly he told her: "I didn't meet anyone who could hold a candle to you!" He pressed his lips to one silky, golden-brown shoulder. "Not even near," he murmured.

Marisa rested her cheek against Jack's hair and was silent. She reflected in quite a self-possessed way that, although it was not a confession of celibacy, it was nevertheless rather nice ... then chased from her mind a thought ... still no mention of love. The thought fled, and she would have relaxed further, but she became aware he was tightening his grip around her. Harder and harder he pressed her against himself, until a protest escaped from her lips. *"Jack!"*

He released the vice-like encirclement but he grasped her upper arm with his right hand.

"Now listen!" His tone was urgent, and he drew back, to regard her face. She met the brilliant hazel eyes with her own bright stare, waiting, lying still and saying nothing.

He gave her a little shake. "You were lonely. You didn't know if I'd be back and I get it! But *there's to be no more of Piers!*"

The name of the man who had been such a dear for many long months struck Marisa's consciousness with a real shock, and it was a painful moment. Piers, with the most dignified of efforts, had hoped to win her heart in the end.

For barely a second, her gaze fell, with curly lashes a veil. In reality her decision was made a long time ago. This younger man brought her excitement and passion; he was the one who owned her heart. The way he had removed himself for so long, bizarrely, had been the only thing keeping her almost trapped in a relationship with Piers, rendered weak by anguish and fear that he'd never return, coupled with her hatred of loneliness. If Jack had not left a year ago, Marisa would have stayed by his side and never faltered.

Poor Piers. Marisa was sure *she loved Jack more.* He was here at last and she felt lucky, as she had known she would. She glanced up at him again. He laughed and tucked a forefinger beneath her chin to raise her mouth to his.

"Those days are over," he told her. "Any time we see him again — no kisses, no touches, no nothing! *Just me.* Okay Maris'? It has to be me, now."

FIN

When I was a child, I spake as a child, I understood as a child, I thought as a child: but when I became a man, I put away childish things.
1 Corinthians 13:11-13 (King James Bible)

SONGS FOR MARISA

Two Door Cinema Club – What You Know
Mumford And Sons – The Cave
The Kooks – Always Where I Need To Be
The Beatles – Don't Let Me Down and Girl
Simply Red – Stars

PART TWO

Honey and Archie

A Meeting

In a market town in Essex, the street outside Honey's flat began to get busy by seven o'clock each morning. Often, she emerged even sooner from the building's entrance, to cross the quiet road and head for a nearby kiosk, where she invariably bought a bottle of water and a cereal bar. Then, she made her way to the sports hall where she worked as a fitness instructor.

On a day that began with no warning that something important was about to happen, Honey wore a thin cagoule over her navy-blue tracksuit, and walked quickly through drizzling rain. Her bright pink umbrella caught a gust of wind and threatened to turn inside-out. Honey sidestepped a deep puddle and paused beneath a bus shelter while she let raindrops fall from her brolly onto the wet path, and tried to adjust it more safely.

An elderly woman was closing and fastening her own umbrella, and once it was tucked neatly in a matching cover, she stowed it inside her handbag. She put out a gloved hand to hail an oncoming bus. "Don't get that pretty hair wet, dear!" she remarked. Honey smiled at her before walking quickly on.

A striped awning over the kiosk was dripping with rainwater, and a light still glowed above it. There were two other customers approaching. One, was a short man dressed in orange overalls and a flat cap. He bought a bacon roll, ready-wrapped in clingfilm, and coffee, which was handed to him in a cup with a plastic lid. He hurried away.

Deliberating over the news stand, a broad-shouldered man stood with his back towards Honey. Clutching a paper, he turned just as she pulled a purse from her pocket and when she opened it – trying to manage without closing her umbrella in case it jammed again – she dropped several coins. The man stopped them rolling away with his foot, then stooped to pick up the money, getting wet fingertips. He placed the coins on the counter for her. Thanking him, she had an impression of dark good looks and a wide, white smile.

Honey stowed her drink and oat bar inside her shoulder bag and was nearly ready to leave, but she stood on the pavement for a moment, sheltering beneath the awning, her eye caught by headlines on the news stand. Reading, she gave an exclamation. A storm had brought down a giant tree, and a couple of passers-by had narrowly escaped disaster.

"That was some kind of luck they had!" The man who saved her scattered coins responded.

Honey frowned over the picture. "It seems worse when something bad happens near my flat," she said. "I know it shouldn't really make a difference, but there's something more shocking about it."

"Yeah," he nodded. He was turning up the collar of his leather jacket. "I guess you live near that big park then?"

"Mm." There was no need to say where she lived. Rain was driving from Honey's right and getting into the unprotected space beneath the awning, and it was beginning to soak her shoulders. She raised the umbrella which she had been holding loosely at her side, pulled it down low over her brow, then briskly walked away.

* * *

Honey normally travelled to and from the sports centre at a jog, often without noticing much of the world around her. She wore wireless headphones, listened to music and stared straight ahead, as she followed a route she knew well after almost five years of making her way to and from the same workplace.

A week or so after the rainy day, the weather changed as the month of June approached. Crossed the road, Honey saw a lorry driver waiting at the lights lean forward in his seat. He raised a hand and smiled at her, with a broad display of white teeth. It was the man who had spoken to her, briefly, at the kiosk. She returned the smile but did not wave.

On a third occasion, their chance meeting was a different matter. Honey had slowed her pace to a walk, and she was obviously limping. The driver pulled the lorry into the kerb and pushed open the passenger door to call out to Honey. Was she okay?

Honey glanced at the side of the lorry and saw a logo she recognised as belonging to a local timber firm. "Uh, well, I tripped … I went over on my ankle!" she admitted. "I'll recover!"

"It's another half-mile to the park!" He remembered their brief exchange. "Do you want a lift?"

Honey's ankle was hurting. He was right about the distance ahead, and she decided to accept the offer of a ride. She managed to hop up the side of the lorry despite her sore foot, and when he reached out a hand to help, she grasped it. Sitting up very straight on the passenger seat, Honey liked it.

"This is … high!" she exclaimed, gleeful as a child. She would never have known, before this, how it felt to be in a lorry, elevated compared to pedestrians and even car drivers below.

"I'm Archie," said her companion, casting her a sideways glance. He wore a black tee-shirt which bore the logo displayed on the vehicle. "And you are …?"

"Honey," she told him. She put up a hand to the cloud of brown hair that framed her face, and turned to give him a smile. She watched the road ahead through the windscreen. "We're nearly there already!"

Archie stopped the lorry near a set of tall iron gates. "Here?"

"Brilliant, thanks!" she said, darting him a look from sparkling brown eyes before opening the door.

"Take care now!" He changed the gear and checked his rear mirror, then watched as she scrambled out of her seat and lowered herself cautiously to the ground. "That name – it really suits you!" he said, then Honey slammed the door, he revved the engine and was gone.

HONEY

Honey lived with her parents when she was very young, but when she was fifteen, her Nigerian father separated from her mother, Linda, and disappeared from their life. He left them in debt and could not be traced, although he had seemed a decent enough man and harmless, if introverted, up until that time.

Linda struggled at first, but she tackled the bills with courage and common sense, and arranged for some of them to be written off. A trained nurse, she managed to maintain her career with the help of a kindly neighbour, who was prepared to look in on her daughter if shifts were late or over-long.

The only child of the tall, black man and the slightly-built, white British woman, Honey had wonderful skin, with a bloom like a dusting of coffee powder. She had brilliant, dark eyes and a cupid's bow mouth. Her mother was very proud of her daughter's beauty, tried her best to provide pretty clothes and accessories, and wanted her to be confident about her appearance.

When Linda met Simon, who worked in offices at the hospital where she nursed, he seemed an uncomplicated individual. He was lean, with untidy brown hair and freckles all over his face and arms. He wore spectacles, was a little bookish, and had every appearance of being trustworthy.

Unfortunately, he was not thoroughly pleasant. It was a painful time for Honey, who was just eighteen when Linda remarried. Simon turned out to have a sarcastic tongue. The fact that he kept knocking her back, ridiculing her exam successes and wondering why she wanted to "swim and jump around" for a job instead of planning a "proper" career, was not entirely lost on Linda, who tried to minimise such harshness. She reproved him mildly, and made efforts to take the sting out of his words by adding her own comments in support of her daughter.

Simon had an undemanding job but he seemed to have a perception of himself as an academic. He affected an interest in philosophy, listened to erudite radio programmes and held forth on subjects he had grasped only slightly.

Linda did not mind all this. She seemed relieved to have a partner. She never discussed aspects of history, politics or philosophy herself and lived from day to day, kindly looking after her patients and engaging herself in practical tasks in her free time. Since she did not offer any argument against Simon's silly theories, he remained contented in their relationship but he clearly saw Linda's more dynamic, less tolerant daughter as a challenge. He was far from being a suitable stepfather for Honey and by the age of nineteen, completely exasperated, she was ready to leave home.

While she attended university, she lived in student accommodation, for a time. The experience made her feel freer. A self-possessed individual, she was not lonely and began to realise her ability to create a routine she enjoyed, socialise when she needed company and be essentially independent.

Honey determined never to try to share home life with her mother and stepfather again. She kept in touch with her mother but would not conceal the fact that she had no time for Simon.

With hard work and a sensible approach to seeking advice if she came up against a difficult course module, Honey got through examinations and gained a degree. She found employment in the sports centre of the town near the university. Linda seemed fairly happy; she didn't question her daughter's decisions and accepted her absence, although they spoke often on the telephone.

Honey taught swimming and aerobics and she helped to supervise the gym. In addition, part-time, she studied nutritional therapies and developed her passion for physical fitness. Since she practised what she preached, she looked and felt very strong.

* * *

Another day brought overcast skies and a forecast of rain. Even though it was June and dawn came increasingly early, the morning was so dark, Honey overslept and found herself with only a few minutes to get to work. She cursed herself for forgetting to set her alarm, but hurried through her morning routine, dressed hastily and left the flat as soon as she could. She began to run really fast, knowing it was her best plan since the block was not on a bus route.

Driving in the same direction, Archie spotted her and saw how quickly she was travelling on her long legs. He overtook, then drew into the kerbside. She pushed herself still harder, ran up to the lorry and peered at him when the door swung open. He said nothing, but he grinned widely.

"Archie! I'm late! Are you going to give me a lift?"

He was. He said, she looked like she was going even faster than usual. He pressed the accelerator, they moved off, and Honey felt better. She would be at the sports halls within a few minutes this way.

"I'm usual well-organised!" She smiled at Archie, who was driving carefully. He had a handsome profile. "I don't often sprain my ankle, or run out late!"

"No," he glanced at Honey briefly. "I figured you were pretty together! Do you need to take it easy sometimes? How did you hurt your foot?"

"No," she rubbed her ankle, remembering. "I'm okay. I didn't actually *sprain* it, not really; it got better quickly. I just slipped on a bit of broken paving …"

He nodded, accepting this explanation.

"I'm a fitness instructor!" She decided to elaborate, lest he thought her an airhead … she'd fallen, she was late … "I teach people that being healthy makes everything else fall into place!" She said this with deliberate irony, and watched his expression.

He got the joke. "Ah!" He grinned again, momentarily, making creases appear around long-lashed eyes. "Well," he resumed a fairly serious manner, and even seemed somewhat thoughtful. "It is good to keep fit, I guess."

After that, Honey and Archie acknowledged each other each time their paths crossed; nevertheless, she would often wave him on, preferring to jog as usual.

A fortnight passed after her late morning and Honey would not have thought of anything in particular to say, had anyone asked if she knew Archie – except that he seemed a nice person – but when she saw him waiting for her, standing near the kiosk and clearly looking out for her, she smiled and felt pleased.

"I wondered if I could walk with you?" asked Archie. "If, that is, you aren't tearing along like something's chasing you?" He had bought a cereal bar for her. Disarmed, she agreed.

So, they walked, and Archie asked about the classes she ran and what advice she might give someone who was struggling with weight issues. At that, Honey regarded him doubtfully; he was a well-built man of medium height and not a bit too heavy. "Not me!" he exclaimed, seeing her stare.

Honey kept a bundle of leaflets in her bag; she fished them out and handed several to Archie. She was not sure how serious he was. Despite the reflective air that came and went, he looked exceptionally humorous most of the time. He smiled readily. The sports hall was some distance from the precinct, and walking it took some time, but they chatted or fell into friendly silence, and were content. They drew level with the front of the sports centre at last.

Archie folded the brochures and stuffed them into the pocket of his jeans. He hadn't referred to them during the walk.

"Thanks for these," he said. He didn't turn away. She waited. "I like your hair," he told her. Honey raised her eyebrows, and he smiled. "I mean, some joggers seem to make their hair flip around ..." Honey could picture those ponytails. He went on, "You don't do that, and your hair ... it's nice!"

Honey's hair was a mass of small, soft, brown curls which framed her oval face and lent depth to her large dark eyes. Today, a wide band kept her hair off her forehead. The curls did move, softly bouncing, when she ran, but no, they didn't *flip*. She wasn't offended.

Well, perhaps she had guessed the man was interested in her. Honey was young but she was self-aware. In a friendly way, she patted his sleeve then adjusted her bag on her shoulders and was about to leave him. Archie seemed reluctant to let her go, and he accompanied her for a few paces and was silent as they slowly crossed the car park. She would have walked away, crossing the last few yards up to the halls to enter through glass doors, when he said, "I like your style!"

Now Honey raised a hand, palm facing towards Archie, in another small gesture, but this time she meant, desist! She shook her head, reproving but friendly.

"I've run out of words!" he admitted.

Just as well! Honey thought, but she smiled, revealing small, even white teeth. "Uh huh, well, see you soon ..."

Archie lingered still. Would Honey meet him the next day, he wanted to know. Would she walk with him? "There's more I want to say to you, if it's okay Honey?"

Wondering if her new friend was something of a Lothario (how could he be oblivious to his own dark-eyed charm?) Honey nevertheless calmly agreed. She would be open-minded, and listen to whatever it was he was storing up, to say. There was nothing about him to cause concern, but, since they barely knew one another, she would meet him at the gates of the nearby public gardens and then they would walk through the town.

It was time to head for the gym. "I'll be late!" Honey exclaimed. She walked swiftly away with her hair a gold-lit halo in the early sunshine. Archie took a step forward, raised both hands in an involuntary gesture almost as if he hadn't known she would leave. Then, he let his arms fall to his sides, standing there for moments more, on the path.

STRAWBERRY ICE CREAM

After work, Honey walked slowly downhill, making her way along the path that ran beside a wide road. Tree-lined, it was pleasant and for the second time in her day she did not rush. Thinking about Archie, on her way to meet him, yet she was considering whether she ought to do this deliberately. He seemed friendly and not threatening in any way. Honey liked people who made her smile, but she was used to being by herself and had no plans to change that, at least not for now. Perhaps the experience of watching her mother suffer when Honey's father left home, and then the feeling that Simon was not right for Linda and yet she would settle for him, had affected Honey and made her wary of relationships.

Her mind flitted between opposing thoughts. Archie was personable and funny, and already they got along well. Honey liked him. Despite this, she wondered if, after all, she could open up her life to a new person. Complicating the second train of thought, was another worry. Surely, he was much older than herself?

There was an ice cream van parked near the iron gates of the public gardens, and she joined a queue of youngsters to buy a cone. "D'you want a flake?" the vendor asked.

"Yeah!" Honey nodded, and scattered coins on the narrow counter.

He fished chocolate from an open cardboard box with a gloved hand. He looked at her with a twinkle in his eye, and passed some change down from his window. "Have a nice day!"

"What am I doing?" she wondered privately. "I don't seem all that decided, and I almost never eat sweet things!"

It was not hard to work out that she really wanted to wait for Archie. She wandered away from the van and the jostling children, and sat on a bench facing the road.

"Honey!" He was there, walking quickly, arriving from somewhere to her left. He looked different. Out of his worn leather jacket and blue jeans, now he was dressed in a loose, brown linen jacket which flapped, unbuttoned, over an open-necked shirt, worn with pale trousers and soft soled shoes. He looked like a character in a film, the opening scene perhaps, a man looking for someone – looking for Honey. He joined her.

"I knew you would wait!"

Honey thought he sounded a bit triumphant. She felt sensitive, because she had been in a quandary. She frowned. "You did not!"

"Hah! You can't be cross – not properly – with strawberry ice cream on the tip of your nose!"

He brushed her nose with his thumb and leaned down to kiss her cheek. "I *did* know you would wait, anyway!" He took her hand, beaming. The kiss was just a brush of his lips, and Honey had been suspecting he had Italian heritage in any case. He might have some different ways, according to his culture. Still, a kiss felt just a little startling. His cheerful friendliness was irresistible.

They walked together, past the wide, open gateway, and on, slowly, taking a curving route into the town. Through railings, Honey could see a playground where children were energetically swinging or sliding. Two little girls danced, holding hands, on the bandstand and dog walkers paraded their pets.

They chatted in a casual way. Earlier, Honey had described her love of swimming, and she elaborated on her plans. She wanted to gain extra qualifications as a lifeguard, as many as possible. Archie talked about a town in Wales, where he often took deliveries of building supplies, and he said there were valleys nearby which were worth visiting, just for the scenery and in some areas, the sea. Sometimes, he said, he drove to France, too.

They were enjoying each other's company, but Honey wondered why he had invited her there. He had said there was "more to say" and she didn't think it was going to be an entirely casual meeting. When Archie's mobile phone shrilled an alert, he stopped walking. *"Sorry ... "* he said, and pulled it from his pocket. Honey waited, and, for reasons she had not identified, was unsurprised when he said he would have to leave her.

"Honey, I thought I had an hour to talk! Forgive me, I will see you again soon." He grasped her hand for a moment, then he left her, walking quickly with his jacket still flapping open, running a hand through his black hair and holding the phone to his ear as he went.

* * *

At the age of almost forty, Archie was – as Honey, of course, spotted – extremely fit and attractive. He was forced to sit in his cab for hours, when his job led to long-distance drives, but he had a lean frame. His dark and handsome looks were inherited from an Italian grandfather; he had a slight accent when he spoke, and with a personable manner too, he seemed more suited to a role on a stage or film set. Honey could not know it yet, but he was a man full of deep emotions.

POSSESSIONS

Despite her difficulties, Linda had always made sure her daughter was well-dressed. She quietly made sacrifices in order to be able to choose pretty things for Honey and, while she was growing up, the little girl felt equal to her schoolfriends.

Now, with an income that covered her needs and created a significant extra amount to spend on treats, Honey could enjoy shopping for herself. She had no need to send money to Linda, who was still working and seemed to remain happy with Simon, who helped her pay the bills.

With summer weather turning out to be wet disappointingly often, Honey hunted online for a smart, rainproof coat. She wanted a garment with neat buttons and a belt at the waist, and soon found the perfect style. Made of soft, expensive gabardine, it was neatly fitted, had a hood and was in a buff shade which flattered her skin and hair. It was nice to wear something different from her tracksuits!

On an afternoon of light, persistent rain, Archie drove slowly, negotiating his way past parked cars, passing along the road near the iron gates on his way home. Spotting Honey, he lowered his side window, so she should hear him call out to her. "Hey!" He smiled and waved.

Honey saw the lorry, saw Archie waving and heard his call. He checked his mirror, and drew up. "Want a rainy-day ice cream?"

The van was parked there as usual, but Honey shook her head. "No thanks!"

She hesitated, standing on the path, allowing Archie time to find something to say that would interest her. She had not seen him since the walk that seemed abruptly cut short but she bore no grudge. She expected nothing from him.

He raised a forefinger. "Hang on!" He drove a little further along the road, and parked in front of a stationary vehicle, then climbed down to the pavement to stand with Honey. Already, she was admitting silently to herself that it was very nice to see him again.

He put up his hands and adjusted Honey's hood. "Cute," he said. "Like a glamorous schoolgirl!"

She chose not to complain that he was being patronising, since, by now, she knew he sometimes made statements that were mildly cheeky. She had not reacted when he joked about her speed *en route* to work, and she would ignore his "schoolgirl" comment. A strong person can assess a situation without immediately declaring it unacceptable, and Honey liked Archie's ways. Flirtatious? He was, definitely. Also, he was full of good humour, in a way that affected and cheered her spirits too.

* * *

Honey told Archie that ice cream would make her chilly. She was heading for a cafe, to get a hot drink and a snack. She did not feel like making a meal from scratch that evening. Did he want to go with her?

A passing driver sounded a horn when he had to overtake the lorry, although it wasn't especially obtrusive. It was parked close to the kerb, with its engine idling. Hastily, Archie checked where Honey wanted to go, said he would move the lorry "to a safer place" and disappeared.

After a few minutes, they met again and sat together in the

warmth of the coffee shop. It was a good idea, Archie agreed, discarding his jacket and rubbing cold hands together. Lights glowed and customers were beginning to crowd in, seeking a haven as the day outside darkened and was gloomy.

Over coffee, Archie confided something about his life at last. In fact, he was married. At that, Honey sat back in her chair and looked worried, but he hastened to tell her: "I wanted to explain the way things are. The thing is, Honey, my wife is not living with me. She has taken herself off, to live with her sister, many miles away from here, and I'm just … I don't know what's going to happen."

"When did she leave?" Honey wasn't sure what to think. Maybe he should be away, looking for his wife? It was about two months since she left, he went on, and she was very difficult to contact.

Honey ate her toasted panini and was silent. She tried to absorb this information. He watched her expression for a moment. "Could I tell you a bit more?" he asked, tentatively. She thought perhaps it would be useful if he did, and nodded.

So, Archie explained. His wife, whose name was Daisy, had lost interest in life in many ways. She seemed unhappy, but would not talk to Archie or look for ways to feel better – except for overeating, seeming to seek comfort from her food. She had become obese, having piled on weight since their wedding a few years before. She was downhearted, watched television for many hours every day, and only stirred to make meals.

Honey was saddened, but uncomfortable. This was a lot of detail to be given, considering she was a relative stranger. She began to demur.

"Archie …"

"I'm not getting this right!" said Archie. He thought for a moment, before going on. "I should say, she is sad. She was keen to have a big family and could not, and ever since then, all the time, she tries to hide away from the world. She is hurting herself, and …

and I can't stop her."

It was a sorrowful story. Honey thought he was probably relating it to her because of her job and her interest in health and fitness. She was not particularly interested in developing a relationship with him – certainly not to a point where they mattered to one another. Perhaps she need not mind that he was married, and they would continue to be cheerful, chatty friends.

Honey's life was busy and she was usually happy, enjoying being an independent woman. The fact was, she had observed a change in her mother, who so wanted to keep a man close but who – in Honey's opinion – had sacrificed some of her peace and dignity when she married Simon. It caused Honey to think twice about relationships and whether she would ever be able to give up her own freedom, and that diffidence was always there, somewhere in the background of her mind.

She hoped Archie would be able to help his wife and said so, as she pulled on her new coat and tucked her curls inside the hood. She had realised something. "That's the reason you asked for those leaflets!"

"Yes, it's true. Thank you for listening," he said respectfully. Then his expression relaxed. He pushed an escaping curl of hair under her hood with a gentle forefinger, "So, Honey ... I guess I'll see you ..." It was a statement not a question. A kind of warmth seemed to flood through Honey's heart and mind, and it was both an emotional and a physical response.

His words tailed off. Honey didn't complete the sentence for him, and she moved away from his touch, but they parted amicably, nevertheless.

* * *

As time went on, a feeling of closeness developed between Honey and Archie. It could have been avoided, perhaps. To Honey, it *felt* inevitable. They both stopped in the early mornings at the newsagent's kiosk, both made their way along the same route, where Honey's destination was the sports centre but Archie roared onwards in his vehicle for the long drive ahead. If they did not travel together unless she accepted a lift (and sometimes she did), they almost always had an opportunity to wave and often Archie stopped, lowered his window and called Honey for a chat.

There were moments, increasingly, when they looked at each other with serious expressions. Awareness of the significance of the times they shared, was there. But when they spoke, their conversation was not about serious things. Instead, often, each one tried to come up with something flippant or silly, to make the other laugh. Unspoken, so far, was the fact that they really liked each other, coupled with the awareness of his marital status. Acknowledged, was their love of laughter.

At last, Honey faced something. "When he is near me, the air crackles!" she thought. "*Or I do!*" In deference to his sensitive revelations, she kept a certain personal distance, still.

* * *

"I'm glad to see you …!"

"Go 'way!" Honey had little breath for speech. "Archie, quit it, I need to exercise!"

"You can have a lift?" He affected an air of surprise.

"Don't need one …!" She tried to think of off-putting things to say. He was idly bringing the lorry along parallel with the wide pathway, the windows were open and he was calling her from inside. "If you keep crawling along like that, you'll get arrested!" she said, although she hoped it wasn't true. "Plus, you're holding up the traffic …"

"I'm not!" He checked his mirrors. "You'd be warmer?" He was in a maddening frame of mind.

Honey stopped running, and when he halted the lorry properly, she climbed in.

"You like me!" Archie insisted, adopting an air of patient reason. "Honey, you do!"

"Think so, huh?" Honey bent to pull a water bottle from her bag, then wriggled to get comfortable. She would admit only to herself that she was glad of the chance to take a break. She sank gratefully into the seat but made three attempts to fasten her seat belt, each one unsuccessful. "Stupid thing!" she grumbled. "I usually do this okay!"

Archie deliberately misunderstood her. "Dear one," he said, in his voice that was tinged with an Italian accent. "You are not a stupid thing!"

"Tch, not me!" She jabbed the metal pieces together again. "This!"

He took the belt's fastenings with exaggerated care, and slotted them easily into place. Then he persisted. "Like me, *a lot* ...!"

"*No!*"

Archie shook his head with a sigh, assuming tired forbearance. After that, he began to remark on how much they liked one another, all the time.

* * *

Archie's watch bothered Honey! It was strapped to his left wrist, and it looked horribly tight. Why did he wear it like that?

"It is not too tight!"

"Yes, it is!" She opened both her palms. "I can see how tight that is ... c'mon!"

He expelled an exaggerated breath, and pretended to unscrew his arm. He thumped his wrist into her lap, and turned his head to look out of the window to his right, as if his arm was really disconnected from his body.

Honey disregarded his little pantomime. She unbuckled his watch, removed it and gave an exclamation. "Good grief, Archie! Look how white the skin is!" She rubbed the strip of numbed skin with her thumb, then put the watch on him, carefully, so it did not pinch.

"Good grief …!" he echoed hilariously. "Does your mother, or may be your *grandmother* say *good grief?*" Ignoring this, she turned his wrist over, slid the strap into a new position to leave the paler strip free and checked the adjustment with a fingertip between leather and flesh.

He bore it all with good grace, waiting to start the lorry's engine so he could pull away from the forecourt of the sports centre. He was absently watching a couple of crows squabbling over a sandwich crust and seemed unconcerned about Honey's care to fix his watch properly. He had, however, made a fist of the hand that lay on the bare skin of her smooth legs. He was controlling himself, and a more mature woman might have spotted it.

LOVE AND HATE

The age difference between Honey and Archie was around thirteen years. She was a little over twenty-six, and he would be forty in the following January, a fact he occasionally bemoaned. He looked younger, with his tanned face, brilliant dark eyes and a tousled head of jet-black hair. Honey was confident of her maturity but found he was inclined, maddeningly, to patronise her.

When Daisy returned to Archie, he told Honey at once. Their friendship had progressed and with the jokes, the confidences and the fondness they had developed for one another the real likelihood that it might be best ended was not something either one wanted to address. Archie continued to grin broadly upon every sight of Honey. She guessed he was struggling, when he admitted that his wife was not different from before the trip away. Still cross, still overeating, she had difficulty in walking, and continued to refuse any diversion or outing he proposed.

They talked in more depth as time went on, lingering for several minutes after they drew up at the sports centre in the mornings or finding a seat beneath the trees, deliberately making time to drink coffee from plastic cups on the occasions when Archie had to set off, eventually, in a different direction. Meetings at the kiosk had become a habit that was more than chance.

Comments led to interested questions, further discussion and reflections. He offered to show Honey a picture of Daisy, saved on his mobile phone. Firmly, she declined, but inevitably they moved on from their early talks, and there were more revelations. Honey described her sense of upset when her father left home and the way her mother seemed distant, and was cool towards her daughter and the rest of the world.

"She didn't tell me he wasn't planning to come back," she said painfully. "I do get it now; I understand she tried to shield me. At the time, I felt silly and left-out, especially when I guessed the truth. I was only sixteen so I had no idea what to do … I had feelings I didn't get, and no-one else to tell."

"No friends at all?"

She hesitated … "Well, there were schoolfriends. Actually, I did tell Rachel. She was great but only my age. Neither of us knew what was right."

"How did you get through it?"

"I was in the middle of exams. Instead of junking them, I decided to do them well. I caught up with some studies that I hadn't bothered with much before that, and worked hard, so I passed everything."

"Clever!" Archie said, admiringly.

"Well I'm not sure about that," she answered. "Actually, I'm not academic and I would always prefer to swim or run, instead of write! I gave it my best shot and kept on studying, and then went to college, concentrating on sports. I qualified as a lifeguard in my spare time. I guess it's how I got – you know – strong."

Honey described her stepfather and said she disliked him but she wanted her mother to be happy. She felt burdened ever since it was obvious that he was not a genuinely kind person, but how could anyone interfere? She tried to look for positive aspects of Simon's attachment to Linda, saw he gave her mother the comfort she needed. He must have resented Honey and it was unfortunate but perhaps it was something he did not know how to control.

Archie explained something more of his own situation. "I'm struggling to know how to help Daisy. If I don't talk to her, she says nothing, and we can go for hours like that, in a silence I can't seem to crack. The problem is, if I try to make her smile, actually she gets angry and she always says I have no idea how she feels, so then I feel like it's my fault she gets so low. I've made her worse. I hate to fight. I guess I have to let her be, but how I long to go home to … well … you know …" His words tailed off.

Honey could tell he wouldn't enjoy a row, he wasn't the kind of volatile man who lost his temper easily, so far as she could tell. She wondered if anything would make him angry, but she said nothing and he picked up his train of thought again. "We eat, but we don't communicate now, not even about small things and when I realise it's no use trying to make her laugh these days, I don't know what our future will be."

Laughter mattered very much, to Archie; it was part of his whole being.

"It must be very miserable, for Daisy to feel ill all the time," Honey said. "It must also be tough for you Archie. What is that like, when someone *always* says she feels bad and you can't seem to change that?"

This was a sensitive question. Archie sighed, seeming reluctant to try to explain. Honey did not think any of Daisy's misery could possibly be his own fault.

"How could it, Archie? If *nothing* works, not keeping quiet *or* being cheerful?"

"I think I know that really," he answered. "I still try, and she turns away from me …" He caught himself before he said too much, perhaps changed or left out his next revelation about married life and said, instead: "So I feel like … I'm responsible for the sadness. We can't go away on holiday, or dancing, can't go out for dinner because she thinks people stare and watch what she eats. We can't even go for a walk, because she just won't!"

* * *

The lorry travelled along the last part of their homeward route on a fast-darkening evening. Honey had lingered at the sports hall to give a learner an extra swimming lesson. Archie, also late, saw her when she ran over the zebra crossing on her homeward route, and he collected her as was his habit by this time. They stopped at a set of traffic lights, and Honey found herself casting sidelong glances towards him, thinking he was unusually quiet. His profile looked enigmatic. Perhaps he was tired?

Archie seemed to bring himself back to the real world with a deliberate effort. He had been musing over something, and it became clear when he spoke. Would Honey meet him later? Would she go with him for drinks?

He had not suggested they might go to a bar before this. She thought about his married status and said she would not. She did not try to embellish her refusal.

"You could," he urged.

"Don't pressure me!" she told him, warningly.

At that, he grinned, losing the distant air quite suddenly. "This is a love-hate relationship," he chuckled. "Love and hate!"

"Well, it is not!" she answered crossly. "Because it isn't a relationship is it? And there aren't strong things in it, like love and hate!"

Archie fell silent then, and lost the grin. The words had fallen from her lips too carelessly; they sounded harsh, and her argument wasn't funny at all. He watched the lights, they changed to green and he slid the vehicle into gear. Honey closed her eyes for a few moments, trying to let the feeling of defensiveness slip away. She hadn't meant to upset Archie, but when she opened her eyes again, she saw he looked unusually serious. Honey stole another glance. Was she imagining Archie appeared annoyed? There was a tiny muscle working in his jaw, and certainly, for the moment, he was trying to say nothing.

Slowed by rush hour traffic, the lorry had to be halted repeatedly before it could make progress, and Archie's knee moved when he pressed the accelerator and drove the great vehicle forward. For seconds, her eyes lingered on his legs clad in dark blue jeans, and a realisation began to be profound. Archie felt familiar, and everything about him felt … well … *beloved*.

Honey tucked her chin into the collar of her coat. Fearing to see pain in his expression, she kept her eyes on the dark route in front of them, and the lights of passing cars.

Archie faced forwards too, as the lorry shifted and they moved on, but he was frowning as he sought for the words he wanted to say. Belatedly, he countered simply, "It *is* a relationship!" He looked at her briefly, then back at the road ahead and she guessed he was not annoyed, but upset.

The lorry drew to a halt near the flats, where he now knew she lived and Archie switched off the engine. Deliberately, he turned towards Honey. She had begun, nervously, to twist her fingers together in her lap but he reached for her hand, and when, childishly, she tried to bury both hands beneath her legs and sit on them, he tugged her elbow.

"C'mon, Hon' …" He freed her hand and slowly lifted her palm to his bent head, and his lips. His mouth and his face were warm. Honey shivered, all through her body. He let her go, but she wasn't sulking now, and her hand seemed to drift, uncontrolled, to her throat. As if to occupy his own hands, he replaced them both on the steering wheel of the now idle lorry. He sighed, and spoke softly. "A relationship," he said again. "Don't say you didn't get that, a long time ago, Honey."

* * *

Their feelings were acknowledged, but still Honey continued to hold herself apart from Archie's efforts to become closer. She disappeared from her usual pathways, and for several days he looked for her in vain. At last, there she was, jogging, wearing a grey tracksuit and a bright green sweatband around her head.

Archie slowed the lorry and pulled into a layby, then stopped and silenced the engine. He jumped from his cab; and swiftly he strode to catch up. Honey stopped running, and turned to face him.

"I'm missing you!" he exclaimed, and the words sounded tortured.

"I went to see my mother," she told him. A little inclination of her head, and downcast eyes, belied unhappiness. "We usually just talk on the phone …" Archie waited and she enlarged on this, but vaguely. "I could visit for once, because stupid Simon wasn't there!"

She made as if to continue to jog, turning again in the direction of home.

Archie drew his breath in sharply. He pocketed his ignition keys, and would not leave her. In an involuntary gesture, he reached out, and took a step towards her. *"Honey!"* he said her name, and Honey found she couldn't move because again she heard that note in his voice, as if he must force the word out, hurting himself, and tearing up her heart at the same. She looked at his outstretched arms and couldn't fall into them, and wasn't sure why.

He recovered and thrust his hands inside his pockets, jangling the keys, but he echoed her words. "Stupid Simon?"

"Uh … yeah … he married Linda!"

"Your stepdad then?"

"My bad luck! He is."

"Why are you leaving me?" he asked. "I went wrong, somehow?"

"Archie." She faced him again. "I always come back from seeing my mum with a messed-up head! I'm sorry … can we catch up in a couple of days?"

* * *

For two days, then, Archie didn't try to hold Honey up, and he didn't call her phone. At last, on the Friday evening she stopped when she saw the lorry overtake her and come to a halt just a few yards away. She leaned down with her hands on her shins, getting her breath.

The door of the passenger's side swung open. Archie stretching an arm from his place in the driver's seat, patted the one beside him.

"Will you jump in, Honey?"

She was chilly and weary; the day had been full of trials and the prospect of shortening her journey home appealed – as, of course, did Archie's company. She scrambled up the high side of the lorry to collapse inside, where, belted safely she was ready to be borne home.

"There!" He covered her right hand as it lay loosely on her knee, holding it under his broad palm and strong fingers.

She turned her hand fractionally, so that her palm was against his, and relaxed. He released her to get the lorry into gear, then covered her palm again, steering with his right hand. In her relief, Honey was on form; the anxious feelings that lay beneath the surface of her thoughts were hidden and instead of expressing distress, this time she was bubbling over with laughter.

She entertained him with a description of a young woman who could not work the controls on the treadmill and simply stopped running, was conveyed to the end and fell off. In her instructor role, Honey was not supposed to find this funny, and said she had to pick the girl up from the floor, wearing a concerned expression. In the telling, the tale affected her still more and she dashed tears of laughter from her eyes.

Her mirth was infectious and Archie could picture the scene. "I tell you what, I was really down tonight!" he told her. "You made me laugh, you cheered me up! *Oh man!* I love you, Honey!"

She looked into his shining eyes and felt as if her pounding heart turned somersaults.

* * *

Honey jumped down from the lorry and saw that Archie was leaving his own seat. He walked around to join her and this time, he reached for her.

"Oh ..." Honey started to pull back.

"No, baby," he said urgently, and now it was no use trying to keep the cheerful talk going. The look in his dark eyes was almost fierce. They stood close together beneath a great oak tree as heavy drops of rain began to fall and there was a distant rumble of thunder. Two people who had met casually, might have commented on the awful British weather but Archie and Honey didn't care. There were no street lights close by and they were in shadows.

"We'll stand here," said Archie as the rain fell more heavily. He drew Honey to him, and leaned against the trunk of the old tree. "Stay for a minute. I want to ask you something. Come closer, Honey." He enfolded her in his arms, and they were powerful around her. Honey felt weak. "I want to hold you, Honey," he said.

Archie was asking her to share more of her time with him, to find a chance to lie down with him, to be intimate. An affair? "It wouldn't work," she murmured, thinking about the invisible Daisy. Her eyes closed and she rested her head against his chest, but she knew his determination was winning her over, her sensibilities were shrinking and becoming nothing. "How would it work?"

He placed two fingers over her lips and the softness of his touch made her spine tingle. "Hey," he murmured, suddenly tender. He cradled her head, bending to brush his mouth across her brow, then lower to meet her lips and kiss her. "Believe me, Honey. It already works."

* * *

Somehow, although they kissed, standing in an embrace for some minutes, Honey began to tear herself away from Archie. She straightened, and let her arms fall from the warmth of his body beneath the leather jacket.

"I'm going," she told him firmly. "I want to stay, but I need time to think."

"More time, *cara mia?*"

"Yes, Archie. More time."

For a moment more, he held her, and he buried his face against her neck before he found his composure. He was respectful. They walked a few paces together with one of his arms around her shoulders and the palm of his free hand pressed against her midriff where her coat fell open and her sports clothes left her skin bare. Again, they halted, and he moved to let her go, but regretfully, holding both her hands, then her fingers, then walking backwards with his eyes fixed on her face and a smile playing around his lips. So, she left him, and entered her flat alone.

Honey knew she was in love with Archie, and there was no going back.

* * *

After all Honey's mental turmoil, all the longing she now felt to be in Archie's arms again, it was a shock when she followed her usual pathways for the next few days and did not see him once. He didn't call her or send a text, and she gathered her pride and would not try to contact him. While this might have been exactly the space she needed, in order to gather her thoughts, it felt too long ... yes, she asked for "time" ... no, she didn't want to feel abandoned! Honey had a youthful expectation perhaps, and thought Archie might be able to give her emotional space while seeing her, still, on their old terms.

Were they close enough now for her to challenge him? Why did he hold her so close, and so tenderly, then disappear as if into thin air?

Honey's bed was pushed against one wall in her open plan rooms, and it was her haven. It had a frame of dark wood and a deep mattress. She made it cosy and colourful with primrose-coloured cotton sheets, a cream coverlet and several plump pillows tucked into vivid rose-pink pillowslips. The whole thing, which Honey straightened neatly before she left for work each day, was covered with a fluffy yellow throw.

On the third night since she saw Archie, despite settling herself into the bed as usual, she could not sleep properly. She woke frequently with thoughts turning into confused dreams, and disturbing her with visions. When dawn lightened her rooms, Honey sat up on her untidy bed and put her face in her hands. She would put this rough night behind her, and pull herself together.

Refreshed by a shower and a cup of peppermint tea, she donned her lightweight jogging suit and left the flat, with a small purse slung around her waist. Hurrying, she became warm despite the cool air out-of-doors; she unzipped her jacket and let it hang open.

Archie was there. He stood near the newsagent's kiosk, and he smiled as soon as he saw Honey running around the corner. She was breathless after her run and the shock of seeing the man without warning, when she had begun to miss him very badly, made her struggle to find something to say. He proffered a couple of purchases: her water and a plastic slip full of slices of melon.

She felt oddly abashed, but she accepted the items. She stuffed the fruit bag into her purse, and stood, holding the drink. "Thank you for these." She couldn't seem to say more, and the tears that threatened to brim from her eyes did not help.

He was easy-going. "Enough time, Honey?" he asked, simply.

It was relief, but Archie had not been entirely fair; that was a long three days with nothing to tell her where he was. She stayed with him for some moments, without knowing what she needed to say or do. Anxiety had dissipated, but Honey was thrown by the way Archie appeared, with no change in his manner towards her. He took a drink from a can of cola, staring at the traffic, his thoughts taking him into a distant, reflective place.

"I have to go," said Honey. She wasn't at all sure, suddenly, that she could keep angry words from bursting from her. She felt quite insulted by this void, after nurturing such a storm of emotions, and high expectations. "I guess I'll see you ..."

It was an anxious moment. Was the closeness they had begun to share still there? Archie turned to face her. She wore a tiny cropped top above the soft jogging trousers; her midriff was bare, warm brown in colour and silky smooth. Then, he did something that settled it for Honey, making her realise she was immensely vulnerable to his charm. He reached out across the few inches of space between them and, almost without seeming to think about the action, he ran the knuckle of a forefinger lightly from beneath her breasts, down to her stomach. Then he let his hand fall to his side.

It was a familiar gesture, an assumption of entitlement to touch that modern women say they reject. A liberty. Years ago, in the nineteen-seventies for instance, few people would have run away and demanded legal advice over something so sweet, and so seductive. For Honey, who had been in Archie's arms not long before, it was like a lightning bolt, more powerful than his gentle kisses on her brow and lips on the night of the storm, more seductive even, than the closeness of their bodies that night.

A Friend

So, *I love him?* Honey tried to address her feelings. She felt vulnerable with her new awareness. "But he's not free," she worried, burdened inevitably by the knowledge that Daisy existed, despite his assurances that everything seemed to be changing. The woman had returned – even if she was being downright unpleasant to poor Archie. With a certain perception, of course, this was his own problem.

She did what a woman sometimes must do, and contacted her best friend.

"Send me a picture of yourself," Rachel texted back. "I forgot what you look like!"

Laughing, for a joke, Honey did. She got a call and carried her mobile phone into her sitting room which was flooded with afternoon sunlight. "It's about a man," she began.

"Ooh, yeah!" answered Rachel. "What does he look like?"

"He's good looking ... he's part Italian," said Honey, being a little vague for someone who had been looking into melting dark eyes for weeks, and was enveloped in strong arms more recently. "He's got a bit of an accent. *Listen!*"

She spilled out a few facts. Friendship followed by mutual attraction; a wife who disappeared and returned; talks, confidences and questions. Did Rachel think all of this was important at all, to

Archie? Did Rachel think, he was playing around with Honey's feelings? With her love, had come the unwelcome intrusion into Honey's consciousness of her potential for jealousy. The risks she faced unless she could drag herself away from the man.

Her friend was pragmatic. "You wonder if you mean anything to him? He is a man, isn't he? Look at yourself, Honey!" She added in some kind of non sequitur, "Crikey, if I just had your legs!"

Honey laughed. Her pal was a petite redhead, with pale freckled skin, tiny hands and feet and a boyish figure. "You'd look a bit weird!"

Honey was young, but she knew perfectly well that some men were capable of being immensely attracted to a woman, then losing interest just as quickly. Despite her loss of confidence however, she felt sure her times with Archie seemed meaningful, and she let herself be comforted by Rachel's words. She remembered all the little touches. A thumb on her nose tip to smudge away ice cream; the gentle adjustment of her jacket hood, and fingertips – featherlight – drifting down her body. She told Rachel he loved to be near her, and admitted, "I can't keep my hands off him, either! I adjusted his watch strap ...!"

Her friend was nonplussed. "Pardon?"

"Never mind!"

"Well," Rachel recovered her train of thought. "You say, he confides in you, and he clearly doesn't fight you off. Doesn't sound like it's one-sided to me – you've *both* fallen in love! It isn't rocket science Hon'!"

"He lets me down sometimes ..." Honey demurred again.

"In what way?"

"He kind of disappears!" It was a brief expression of painful emotion. She was finding herself feeling the strain of those hours when she was left wondering. Her running helped to calm her nerves, but she had feelings for Archie that were greater than anything else, and nothing in her life compared to time spent with him.

"Often?" Rachel knew what it felt like, to spot that risk of being taken for granted.

No. Considering everything: Archie's long hours of work and his attempts to talk to Daisy fairly, Honey realised it was not often. "I needed to think ... I said, give me more time ..." She broke off. "*Oh!*"

Honey had talked herself into an understanding, and it was clear to Rachel, too. "Well, that would make a good man leave you alone for a while!" she commented, drily.

So, they came to an honest conclusion. Rachel thought Archie must be struggling too. It was inevitable that he would try to support his wife; he would want to do right by her. "If he is as lovely as you say, he must be wrestling with his conscience, too?"

"Well," Honey sighed. "He *is* lovely!"

"Okay! He's adorable, and probably does have a sense of duty ... as well as a detail that sort of matters, Honey!"

"Poor Daisy is obese, and ill with depression."

"Ah," Rachel answered in a tone of compassion, as Honey knew she would eventually. There was a pause. "It's something of a pity you even know her name ... and poor her, after all. There's no easy answer, now you feel like this, Honey!"

Rachel had to go. They ended their call, but her friend's words stayed on Honey's mind. In love? On the night of the storm, when she sheltered beneath the towering tree in Archie's arms, yes, she had realised her feelings had gone so far – but even then, she hadn't understood how complicated this would be.

Still, as it happened, she had told him "No" for the last time.

* * *

On a cool morning, Honey had arrived at the playing field beside the sports centre by the time Archie's lorry rumbled to a halt in the lay-by just ahead of her. She stopped jogging, slowed to a walk and looked up at his window. She had no time, and it was frustrating, but she was about to cross the car park to the entrance of the halls, where the double doors would soon be unlocked and the first class would begin. Once, she would have simply blown a kiss, and gone on. However, now, this seemed impossible.

"Honey!" Archie called.

She would tell him she had a very few minutes to spare. She went over to his open window, knowing it would be seconds before she would find it difficult to turn away. How was it that she felt the warmth of him, from the kerb beside his cab? Why *was* he warmer than anyone else she had ever met, including the sweating men who hit on her any time she went dancing? He opened his door and swung his legs around, to sit sideways on his seat. She put her arms up to him, and they grasped one another's hands.

"Daisy moved out," Archie told her. "She didn't even wait until I got home yesterday and all her things have gone from the bedroom! She's taken stuff from the bathroom … from the wardrobe … her shoes …" He sighed. "She's got loads of those!"

"But she left before, right? Perhaps it's not for long?"

"Uh, well, she didn't seem to take much last time!" He tried to smile.

Had he called Daisy? "I tried all evening but I couldn't get anything back," he admitted. "She sent me a text this morning. She's at her sister's house, Honey – it's miles away from here!"

"What will you do?"

He pressed a thumb and forefinger to his eyes and slowly raised his head, looking tired. His thick, black hair stood on end; he had been running his fingers through it. He said, "I think I will just let her be, for now. I feel sort of useless. I don't even *know* what she wants me to do!" Just for a moment, he stopped speaking; then, on a questioning note, he finished, "Hon' …?"

His eyes were on her face, and the little word sounded like a term of endearment. Honey had no idea what Daisy wanted. She did not know this person, who was said to have been so pretty and graceful once but lost her self-esteem so completely that she rejected her dark-eyed, fun-loving husband. Daisy had been especially ill-tempered lately, saying sharp things to Archie; he was already at his wits' end.

She held his hands more tightly, and he raised their clasped fists and kissed her knuckles, one at a time, lingering. Honey lost her train of thought for some moments.

"Maybe you are right, to let her be?" His lips were making her feel weak, but she tried to say something wise and ploughed on. "I guess, Daisy felt a need for a bit of space." She sighed, became conscious of her lack of time and pulled away from him. "Sorry, Archie."

For a minute more, he would not let her walk away. "Will you talk to me later?" he asked urgently. "Come for drinks, just one or two, and an hour of your company? Will you, Honey?"

"Archie, I …" She wanted to accept and the longing to support him was powerful, but how was it her place? *A married man?* Even though he seemed to have been left, summarily, to his own devices!

Honey spent long evenings alone in her flat. She had formed habits which used up her time. She ate lightly after work, sometimes indulged in a bubble bath, and got on with her study of nutritional therapies. She enjoyed her career and the attempts she was making to build on the education already behind her, but it *was* a solitary life. A change, just for one evening, was tempting. In any case, she had been in Archie's arms, she had returned kisses. She felt as if she was conscious of the beating of his heart even when she wasn't really close to him. It was surely too late, to refuse.

So, Honey said she would meet Archie and, despite misgivings, the day sped past as she took her classes through their routines with part of her mind on how things would be, and also, since she was only human, on what she would wear.

* * *

When Honey walked into the bar they'd selected as a rendezvous, heads turned and admiring glances were directed towards her. She moved with dignified ease, light on her feet in a pair of delicate, high-heeled gold sandals, not exceptionally tall but slender and so upright. She wore a yellow dress that clung to her toned form and left her knees and lower legs bare. Bracelets gleamed on her wrists. Her hair, with its gold and brown curls, shone. She looked more sophisticated than any other woman there.

Archie, seated on a tall stool at the counter, was staring into his drink but when he heard another man whistle on a low note, he looked up. Honey turned her lovely head to seek him out amongst the drinkers and her face lit with pleasure when he stood up. She crossed the room to join him. Archie kissed her cheek and was enveloped in her fragrance, which, faintly reminiscent of oranges, was light but seductive.

They ordered wine, then, clasping their glasses, they moved away from the bar. The evening was chilly and the landlady had lit a fire, which crackled pleasantly. Stepping past a sleeping lurcher, they found a double sofa, where they sat, leaning against floral patterned cushions, beginning to relax. Their eyes locked; they were delighted now they were, quite deliberately, together.

"I was going to tell you my troubles," said Archie. "I've changed my mind! Honey, you look very pretty; let's forget my stuff and talk about your day." If Honey had really thought to maintain a simple situation, now she hadn't a hope!

* * *

With the disappearance of Daisy, for both Archie and Honey there came a sense that he was free. He had been left without warning, without plans or proper communication, and he would do as he pleased. Now, with that calculated removal of herself and her problems, inevitably his wife left his way clear – and it led to a deeper entanglement with Honey.

However, for this occasion, Honey had taken the precaution of ordering a taxi to take her home, and she told him as soon as they sat down together. He accepted her choice, respectfully. Later, when the car arrived, he left the pub at her side, and they walked across the parking area.

Honey was holding his hand. "Goodbye Archie," she said.

He gave her a gentle kiss on her mouth, and a hug, then opened the door, stood back and let her go. "I will see you soon, then, Hon' ..." he said.

A Meal

Archie had become hopelessly uncertain about his future with Daisy but he had a strong sense of moral duty. She continued to be absent, and at last he offered to travel to the north of the country to see her. However, she rejected this idea and insisted it was better for her to be in a different environment, with her sister.

Fighting heartache, he turned again to Honey. Parked beneath trees on her route home, he sat in his cab and read through a collection of recent text messages from Daisy, before switching off his mobile phone. With an impatient gesture, he threw it into the glove compartment in front of him. He leaned back in his seat and stretched his arms above his head for a moment, watching for Honey to appear in his rear-view mirror. and as soon as she was there, he leaned over to his left and pushed open the door. Her vivid face appeared at the passenger side of the lorry.

"It's no use, Honey!" he told her without preamble. "I really think she might stay there now. She seems so ... flat. Not like her old self." He looked strained, and Honey got into the lorry. "Come here!" he said in a voice rough with emotion, and it was an order, and she did not mind. She put her arms out to him and was enveloped in his powerful bear hug. She was right, Archie's typical frivolity had gone.

After holding Honey very close for a moment, Archie released her and she clipped herself into her belt. He reached for her hand and kept it tucked into his elbow, shifting every now and then when he had to change the gears. While they waited at traffic lights, an old lady pottered slowly across the road, her tiny dog lagging behind as it moved stiffly. Honey was barely aware of the scene and glancing at Archie, saw that, while the lorry waited, his eyes were on her face, with a potency that stirred her into a fearful excitement.

They moved on, the engine roaring as they picked up speed and he was watchful, now checking the road ahead, now glancing at Honey again. Before long he halted the vehicle and leaned at once to cradle her with his left arm, and lay the palm of his right hand on her belly. Honey wasn't alarmed now. It was obvious that with her acquiescence, he was becoming impassioned … and for her part, she was suffused with desire, ready to match him with longing. When she relaxed and accepted her closeness with Archie, instead of scowling in an attempt to convince him she hated his behaviour (he never thought that), their shared times were wonderful.

"Alright Archie," at last, she said. "Come to the flat this evening, and I'll make a meal for both of us."

* * *

Honey stopped trying to analyse her every response and went ahead with plans for a meal she hoped Archie would love. It was fun to shop for ingredients she rarely bought as a rule and as soon as she arrived in her flat with bags full of groceries, she switched on her oven and began to cook.

She made a rich steak and kidney pudding with thick gravy. To serve alongside it, she boiled new potatoes and peas, to which she added butter and mint. A couple of large field mushrooms were sliced and gently fried with garlic. When Archie arrived, looking crisp and smart in a pale blue shirt and a pair of light trousers, he gave her a hug, then beamed as he entered the room. "I can smell something good!"

Archie drank lager while she finished her preparations but Honey sipped only water, afraid to make herself feel too relaxed at first, since she rarely cooked a meat dish and needed to watch her timing! When they ate, she shared each dish, taking small portions but Archie ate well. He observed her modest plateful and smiled. "I'm thinking you made the food with me in mind!" he said. "Thanks, Honey!"

"No, I like to eat meat sometimes," she answered. "I burn a lot of calories anyway ..."

"Yep, all that running!"

"I love it," she told him. "It makes me happy!"

Happy. Archie looked at her vibrant face, the beautiful arching brows above sparkling brown eyes, the curly lashes and full mouth. She brimmed with health and vitality.

After they finished eating, Honey collected a bottle of wine and fresh glasses from her kitchen, and Archie began to confide some of his deeper feelings. He described something of the hurt and disappointment in a marriage that held joy and promise in its early days but became tainted, cloying and life wrecking, really, because Archie could neither mend matters nor be free.

Trying to explain, he was animated, leaning forward and waving his hands expressively. His eyes looked luminous, so much passion was in his words. He made efforts to be fair to his wife, and yet it was his heartache he revealed. "Daisy was everything to me and I admired her. When we met, I was just a lad who was content to drive lorries – I'm three years younger than she is. I couldn't believe it when she agreed to marry me.

"She liked to go to church and I would go too, just because it meant so much to her. At first, I didn't mind it and that was all, but I got to quite like some things ..." He didn't elaborate. Returning to Daisy, he went on, "She seemed like a creature from another world, a goddess, to the kid that I was then ..." He thought for a moment, then continued. "It was because of the way she moved ... I think. She was tiny, but she walked as if she was on air, somehow. She looked after herself and was always smart. She put on little suits, wore high heels, and her hair was very neat and sort of silvery."

Listening, Honey could visualise this somewhat conventional, feminine woman. She waited to hear more about the change in Daisy

"She wanted to have children and after lots of hard times – so much disappointment for poor Daisy – she began to be depressed. The problem was, you know, not her *fault* but it lay with her, not me." He tried to be fair. "I mean, I'm not surprised she was hurting, but we needed to move on together. Instead, she ate, stayed indoors, watched the television. She gave up on stuff she used to love. She used to do her nails, always pink and kind of shiny.

"She didn't give up on food though. Now, she won't let me see her body, or make love to her even in the darkness. She makes excuses to get into bed before me and I know she pretends to be asleep when I go into the bedroom." He put his hands to his temples, pressing with fingertips for a moment. With a sigh, he said, "I don't think God wants us to do nothing but exist!"

Honey had no religious faith, but she loved this emotional man with all her heart by this time, and she was moved. Daisy's story sounded sad, but if she had a Christian faith, why wouldn't she honour her husband, and share comfort, no matter what happened to them?

Honey shared Archie's belief in the vibrancy and value of life. She knew she was fortunate never to have faced anything so awful that she risked losing all her enjoyment of things that mattered. Her face fell serious as she watched his changing expressions and she reached out, to lace her fingers with his.

Archie was suffering beneath his cheerful exterior, and it was clear he really thought he was facing the end of his marriage. He shared red wine with Honey and fell silent. They slipped into a companionable peacefulness, and he seemed to feel better. The light began to fade but they sat on at the table, neither one moving to turn on a lamp, beginning to make each other's face out only in darkness. It felt like the start of something new between them now, and they continued to hold hands across the table top but strangely they didn't feel the need to rush.

It might have been such a different evening – how was it that they could bring Daisy's plight into the conversation and yet still feel their time together was all about them? Why didn't they abandon thoughts of food, for the love that was to come? These were questions for another day, when Honey might reflect on all that she had done, and perhaps remember how sure she was on this special evening, of her love, and of Archie's feelings too – believing he was about to show her he loved her very much.

When Archie stood up and stepped across the space between them, Honey stood too and he took both of her arms to bring them around his waist. She did not argue but let him draw her near and held him as he dropped kisses all over her smiling face.

* * *

Archie stayed with Honey all night, thrilling her with his adoration and his tender lovemaking. In the morning, she watched him while he slept on, looking peaceful although the frown lines between his eyes were deep. She admitted to herself that she had been looking for his company for a long time. Meetings were only partly by chance, since she could have followed different pathways, and she felt compassion for this man who so loved to be happy, and to be supportive of the people he loved.

At twenty-six, Honey had scant experience of the way sorrow makes people behave, but it was not hard to imagine how Daisy's silence and disinterest must affect her husband. He was far more sensitive than his façade of cheerful bravado revealed. Honey thought about loss, and her mother. She remembered how low in spirits Linda was, after her divorce.

When Archie awoke, he reached out for Honey again and found her there, waiting to fall back into his arms.

At last, they began to face the reality of their day. Dressed and with Honey's bag packed and thrown down by the door along with Archie's leather jacket, still they lingered, drinking coffee and postponing the moment of parting. They stood at the kitchen counter, pouring fresh cups, spooning brown sugar, talking about their work, about places they had visited, and sometimes bringing memories of childhood into the conversation. They were happy, in a way, and loving, and Archie wanted to give Honey kiss after coffee-flavoured kiss. It was going to be hard to separate when those few more precious minutes had slipped by. Still, the invisible force that was Daisy was also present.

Honey had something she wanted to explain. "My mother, Linda was similar to the way you say Daisy is. It was a long time ago, when my dad left us. She actually ate too little and she got pale and scrawny, but she did seem to hide, from people, and from life. I was only a teenager but I knew she had stopped taking an interest in the world and I wondered why she didn't smile or have fun, at least with me. You know, Archie, she went to see a doctor. It was after I cried one day, and said I didn't know what to do … I remember she looked at me as if she had suddenly seen me properly for the first time in ages. When I got home from school, she was waiting to tell me what she did.

"She had managed to get herself dressed and out of the house, she got on a bus, and made it – without having one of her panic attacks – to the surgery. She was sort of proud. I made her a cup of tea, and I still didn't really know what else I could do, but she had been given some pills, and you know, she did, slowly, get better.

"I wonder if Daisy needs to see a doctor? Perhaps she is depressed and could be helped?"

Honey was to marvel at herself at a later date! Why had she tried to suggest a way forward for a woman who was really a stranger? Her idea had the potential to lead to the Daisy's recovery! Archie would regain his former life, and – if those things happened – surely a loss of her own would inevitably follow. Honey thought it would be a happier outcome for her, if Archie gave up on his wife. It was a hard train of thought, because her chosen career meant she looked for ways for other people to be well and strong! It wasn't natural, for her, to wish something bad on any couple.

* * *

After Archie left the flat that morning, Honey felt overwhelmed by her emotions. The feeling seemed to come from nowhere but she found herself abandoning her usual routine, losing track of time and, before long, wishing she had let Archie drive her to the sports hall. She wandered around, made fresh coffee and let it cool while she stood, daydreaming, at a tall sash window. Eventually, she decided to abandon attempts to get to work; she would stay at home to give herself time to think. She shook up her bedclothes and crept back between the sheets, and before falling asleep she made just a brief call to the sports centre and told the kind manager she had a headache. It was unimaginative but, as a matter of fact, Honey realised it was the truth.

Honey began to feel conflicted and her thoughts were painful. Indecision was an unwelcome state, because in love with Archie, she wanted to be with him more than ever. She couldn't make her thoughts about his wife vanish, and there was a stark comparison with her old life, and it made her fearful. How could she trust her mother to love her, she wondered, years ago, when Simon was around? How could she be happy with Archie now, knowing Daisy was still dear to him? Such influences were uncontrollable, and they seemed to undermine her happiness,

With the emergence of thoughts which frightened Honey, she withdrew from Archie. For a couple of days, she didn't seek his company, ignored her phone, and kept herself to herself. She thought about him constantly without knowing what to do, but she tried to hide. Was she in this relationship so deeply, it was now impossible to halt the process?

A passionate nature can lead to great love, sorrow and of course, anger. Honey had considered that Archie was so placid he might be that way all the time, but she was inexperienced. It was just one evening and one night before Archie was cross. Honey could tell from his messages, when she looked at them at last, and saw the texts which were first confused, then abrupt and challenging, that she had upset him. They had gone too far, for Honey to justify keeping herself hidden.

She called him, got past his urgent questions and a reproof ("I was worried, Hon'. You can't cut me out like that!") with a lump in her throat. It was a lesson learned; she could not fall in love and then out again, on a whim.

* * *

When Archie returned to her flat, the short time they had been separated turned out to trigger inflamed emotions for them both. They were frantic to be together, and thoughts of anything but lovemaking fled, for hours. Finally, they had to eat, and were forced out of the bedclothes and into the kitchen to find food and make a meal they could share. Archie pulled ingredients from cupboards, and began to boil spaghetti.

Honey tipped olive oil into a pan, diced and fried courgettes, garlic and red onions, threw in a great deal of sliced chorizo and when the mixture had finished cooking and was combined with the cooked pasta, just ahead of serving the dish, she stirred into it a spoonful of cream. With Archie, she ate vast quantities, and they shared garlic bread, but they drank only water and did not want a dessert.

Later, Archie slept. Honey was still wakeful, and she wandered about the flat. She began to tidy the kitchen counters. The leftover pasta, now cold, still looked tempting and she scooped some up with the wooden spoon she had used for stirring. As she raised it to her lips, there was Archie, behind her!

"No!" he tried to take the spoon away. "Stop that! Think of your little hips!"

Honey elbowed him rudely, and refused to part with her extra mouthful. She ran away, cupping a hand under her chin. He caught her easily, but not before she stuffed the great spoonful into her mouth. She sat down on her couch, to deal with it, chewing behind spread fingers, inelegant because she was also laughing.

Archie threw the spoon into the sink and clamped the lid firmly on the pan, with a reproving eye on her. She wiped the corners of her mouth on the back of her hand, and looked back at him, triumphantly. He sat beside her, but his mood had altered. No longer playful, he wrapped her in his arms for some moments.

Honey accepted the embrace, and put her arms around him and held him very close. Soon, he drew back, stared at her in silence, then shifted to lay his head in her lap. She bent to kiss his brow and smoothed his hair with a gentle hand. Their mock fight was over and, content, she reflected it was surely like this if an affectionate bear was trusting enough to cuddle! But Archie was very quiet.

She leaned forward and peered into his face, and was shocked to see there were tears on his cheeks ... *"Ah, Archie!"*

One Thousand Days

Archie went away on a trip to France, and there was no doubt he had to go, but it left Honey feeling lost. She couldn't avoid a thought which seemed to have been waiting to renew itself, and plague her. It was the way he still made efforts to talk to Daisy. They were efforts he did not conceal, but his wife and her illness and her terrible changes of heart were woven into the structure of his relationship with Honey, and she could find a way to be aware of all this, alongside her love for him, when he was near, with his fascinating combination of ego and vulnerability.

Archie would be absent for three days but, as the fourth day wore on and she received no call, Honey began to feel unhappy again.

At last, as she sat in her window after returning from work, drinking tea, disinterested in eating a salad she had prepared and left on the kitchen counter, her mobile phone began to ring. Honey made herself sound calm. "Hey," she said and listened to Archie's breathless voice.

"Honey! I was stuck, in all the traffic, for hours … are you okay? Will you see me?"

At once he was forgiven and soon, he appeared on the path outside, hurrying, looking up to her window and laughing with pleasure when she waved. He ran into her flat when she opened the door, embraced her, lifted her in his arms and took her to her bed.

After they made love, she rested on her back against the pillows, held Archie's hand on her breast and was quiet, feeling sleepy but not ready to sleep. She was aware too that Archie, lying on his side, was watching her. "Are you okay?" he asked her again.

Archie had her heart, he knew it and although she flatly refused to tell him she loved him, there was no hiding her feelings, especially in bed with him. He, on the other hand, expressed his love often and when she lay against his chest, being held in his strong, brown arms, she heard him murmur: "*Ti amo* ... I love you, Honey!"

Honey was aware of a wistful mixture of joy and sorrow. "Archie," she said. "I feel like I will see you this time and then not for *a thousand days!*

"A thousand?" he asked. "A year only has three hundred and sixty-five!"

"Hours, then!" she said, not caring about the mathematics, only about her point. She got lonely.

"Listen!" He raised himself on an elbow. "I'm all done with work – tonight, and all Friday and Saturday too! I can't do any more hours, not allowed, it's a health and safety thing. Honey, get tomorrow off and stay with me! Wait ..."

He leaned from the bed, dug his mobile phone out of the pocket of a jacket slung over a chair and opened the calculator. He cast a measuring glance at Honey, then with exaggerated concentration and pursed lips, he tapped numbers and said, "That's ... hmm ... until Sunday, mid-day, it is sixty-five hours! Okay Honey?"

He was silly but she couldn't help giggling, and she abandoned her irritation to agree to his plans.

* * *

They took first a taxi, then a train, and went to the Norfolk coast. There, they were blissfully happy all day, setting aside every responsible thought, to swim and sunbathe. It was July, and wet weather had disappeared. The sun shone brilliantly and baked the sand, and caused families who had thrown down their rugs and picnic baskets and buckets and spades, to cover themselves with protective lotions. Honey's skin, oiled with a generous hand by Archie, was like toffee. He was difficult about having a sun oil on his body and she gave up, thinking it was up to him.

"Hmm," Honey sighed, raising her face to the warmth and looking through her dark glasses at the sky. *"The sky is blue and I believe it blue but when I see it … it's blue beyond belief!"*

"Sounds like a quote," he took her chin in one hand and turned her face to his, to kiss her mouth. "Dreamy Honey!"

"One of Linda's favourites, I probably got it wrong. I think it's from a film … Oh, you kissed off all my lip-gloss!"

"Your mum sounds nice!"

He left her for a while, climbed steps and went along the seafront to find a shop where he could buy food for their lunch. Honey watched a group of children paddling at the edge of the sea, where wavelets sparkled and gulls floated peacefully a little further from the shore. The sand that stretched in front of her was smooth, washed clean by the earlier high tide.

Honey thought that for her, Heaven would be similar. Around her there were shells and she gathered a handful, absently sorting them into different types and then arranging them on one of Archie's shoes.

* * *

"Something light," ordered Honey when he asked for her choice of snack and he brought her a puff pastry cheeseburger. She ate it uncomplaining; it was a treat of sorts, dripping with tomato sauce, not a healthy snack but hot and delicious.

Dangling from his little finger, there was a tiny toy, a fluffy shocking pink rabbit attached to a keyring. "For you!" he said. "A gym bunny!"

She fixed it to a metal ring on her bag. "Hey! Doesn't *gym bunny* mean something … a bit rude?"

"Not always," he grinned.

"I liked my lunch!" she sank back into the sand, replete. She clasped her hands over her stomach, imagining it had become more rounded, and repeated her thought: "Sinfully good!"

"Like you!" said Archie. "Your skin … it's sinfully good." He stroked her oily stomach with a gentle hand. "*Honey …* a word that sounds like what it means. Sweet, soft, *slippery!*" Then, inconsequentially, "In Italian, *miele …* in French, *miel!*"

"Dope!" she said affectionately. "You speak French, as well as English and Italian?"

"Well, I go there a lot," he answered first but diverted he said, "Hey! did you just call me a dope? I said you were sweet!"

Honey remembered how excited she was in the early days when she thought she must be crackling with it or that the air around her fizzed! Today, she felt contented and secure.

"Now," she decided, "the world is glowing, and I am too!"

Archie wanted to swim but Honey thought the sea looked cold. He teased her: "How can the water *look* cold?" Grey water did look cold, she insisted, and she was nice and warm in the sand. He stood up, pulled off his loose tee shirt and said he would go and test it.

Archie walked away from her. He had on a pair of fawn swimming shorts, and a striped towel was slung around his neck. Honey wished he would simply lie down beside her and stop being so restless, and again, she found herself wondering why Daisy rejected him. His back was broad, muscular but not muscle-bound. His skin colour was a deep tan. He held his head erect, and his black hair lifted and swept across his brow in a sudden breeze. He walked with a purposeful stride and a bikini-clad woman passing by him on the shore looked at him once, then again, in a shameless double-take.

Honey struggled to believe Daisy wouldn't want the man she knew. Hating herself for the thought, she wondered if it was possible that Archie was not as kind as he seemed. Was he different, somehow, towards his wife? The idea felt unlikely. She knew Archie agonised about Daisy. He was only human; he had already tried so hard to find answers, and he was at a loss.

Honey stretched herself out on her rug, lying on her tummy. She dug her fingers into the sand, grabbing handfuls which she let fall, trickling into small heaps full of minute particles and broken shells. Her thoughts ran on, and she dismissed the idea that Archie might not be kind.

In a short walk from the place where their colourful rug was spread out on the sand, on his way down to the water's edge, he stopped when he saw a small boy who was trying to manage a large spade. Archie gestured towards the spade, was handed it, and dug quantities of sand before standing back as the child climbed into the resulting hole whereupon, clearly following instructions, he carefully tipped in a splash of water from a bucket.

Even when Archie ran back to her with his feet thudding over the sand, said she was "shark bait" and carried her, protesting and wriggling, down to the chilly waves, Honey knew he was as good-natured as he seemed on their first meeting on that rainy morning, when they stood underneath a newsagent's awning and marvelled over the lucky escape of a local couple.

With a towel around her wet shoulders, recovering from her dip and a water fight which ended in kisses, Honey ventured a question. How had he coped with the thought that he would not be a father?

"Well, you know, I had three brothers and two sisters, all younger than me! My mother could not look after all of us, she got tired, and she and my dad had very little money. I was sent to live with my grandparents. I loved them, but I felt pushed away from home … I used to try to be good, in case it was my fault, hoping I might go back some day.

"I never want to make a kid feel so bad! I know I could try to make things different, if I had a son ... but I feel better if I leave my past behind. I have some happy memories, of course I do ... I just don't really want to have a family. Daisy doesn't know it, but the sorrow is hers alone."

In response to his honesty, Honey had to deal with an overwhelming surge of compassion, and it hit her for so many reasons. She knew what it felt like, to have memories of happy times tinged with sorrow for the confused child she once was.

Archie so wanted to please his wife, he would have become a parent, never to reveal that it was not truly his wish, and he would have made everything as wonderful as he could for Daisy ... but she was a woman who could not bear a child. Honey wondered why Daisy refused to think about adoption, but she realised how realistic Archie's fear might be – and it must have grown as his life with Daisy had gone on and he saw how downhearted she could become. With a baby to care for, Daisy might *not* find the happiness she believed was dependent only on motherhood. She could lapse into depression and push away her child, just as Archie's mother once did.

With a sigh, Honey brought her thoughts back to the moment. She stood up and let towels slip from her shoulders, and she would have reached for Archie, but he had found his shell-covered shoe. She had to address his entirely unfair accusation that she must have been responsible for putting a shell inside, where it was rolling around in the toe!

* * *

The long day drew to an end and the sands emptied as families began to leave, carrying their possessions and encouraging tired children to follow. Couples like Honey and Archie wandered away slowly, hand-in-hand, leaving behind them the sound of the sea.

* * *

They entered the flat, spilling sand from shoes and bags, which they abandoned at once and by mutual consent headed for the shower, crowding in together to wash away the sand from their glowing bodies. Archie would have gone from the shower to the bed but Honey was hungry!

"I'll get supper," she said.

Supplied with a can of beer, he sat in the last of the sunshine on her tiny balcony while she made a salad with finely chopped onions, whole cherry tomatoes and feta cheese mixed into the crisp lettuce. She poached chunks of salmon and served the meal with a warm baton of crusty bread.

On Saturday, feeling sated with fresh air, good food and love, they drank coffee and needed nothing more all morning, other than the arms, the soft words and the adoration of each other. Later, Archie proposed a walk to the pub and Honey forced herself out of bed, to soak in a bubble bath before she got ready to go with him.

She sat at her mirror to apply mascara and smooth moisturising cream on her cheekbones and the bridge of her nose. She wore a tiny pair of briefs, pure white with narrow black piping on the hem. Archie was still lying on the bed, arms folded behind his head, despite being the one who had suggested they might move. He watched her and she caught sight of his expression, reflected in her mirror. She stood up, and quickly pulled on a white shirt, short-sleeved and a pair of cut-off jeans. Turning her back deliberately, she finished this outfit with simple leather sandals that sparkled with dainty silver buckles; then she straightened, smiling.

Archie expelled a breath with an air of disappointment and a wag of the head, acknowledging her haste and the silent joke between the two of them. He unfolded his arms and sat up, then went off to the shower with an air of mock resignation.

In a few minutes, freshly showered and wrapped in a towel knotted around his waist, he came to her side, and pulled Honey into his arms. Risking his embrace, she let herself lean against him.

"Let's stay here," said Archie. "We'll eat … uh …"

"Nothing!" Honey became practical. "There isn't much food left!" She had a trump card – "and no milk!"

Would they be recognised in the pub? She had begun to convince herself that Archie might set aside any worry about that. Honey was longing for more freedom in their relationship, and hoping, after all, to be the most important woman in his life. For some time, she had known for sure that she was in love and of course, she wondered if Archie might care enough to stay

Most of the customers sharing the bar were interested in the football game, which they watched on a wide screen, set high against a wall. A middle-aged woman emerged from the ladies' cloakroom and passed by their table. Like the young woman on the beach, it was obvious she had an eye on Archie's dark good looks. She trailed in her wake a cloying, musky perfume.

Honey saw the woman stare and she didn't care, but raising expressive eyebrows at Archie she covered her mouth with her hand, hunching her shoulders, acting as if she would choke on the heady mist of old-fashioned perfume. Archie hastily took her elbow, and guided her towards a seat, curved and cushioned, hidden away on the opposite side of the room.

They drank red wine and ate club sandwiches, with their free hands still clasped together. They were glad, simply, to be in each other's company. This was "happiness", Honey thought and she was aware of her feelings as never before, even while nothing more exciting was happening than sharing a lunch. Archie was not abstracted, or going over his worries. He simply ate and drank, held her hand, and seemed content. There was a song playing on the radio; it had been turned down because of the football but was audible from a speaker above their heads and a lyric was:

I'll go wherever you will go.

"That's like us!" observed Archie, and Honey did not argue, despite immediate thoughts of her loneliness when he went to

France or drove far north. In reality, she couldn't go everywhere he did but the sentiment was true, and she was glad he knew nothing of the *Lothario* fear she once had.

When she relaxed, letting Archie be as loving and funny as he naturally was; when she set aside all her guilt and worries and the insistent voice inside her head that warned: *This can't last!* Honey felt happy.

* * *

Happiness can last for some couples, but trying to keep a relationship free of doubt cannot be done in a love triangle. Honey found joy with Archie, and he loved her – but also, he still loved Daisy. With Daisy living separately from him, Honey could hope for Archie's undivided attention, could smother her guilt and believe her happiness would go on. When he told her, he'd been receiving messages from his wife, Honey felt as if she needed to cover her ears. He explained, at first, he'd found a series of texts on his phone, then there came a longer message in an email. Daisy had asked if he would talk to her on the telephone.

"You'll say, you won't …?" Honey hoped, but she didn't say the words aloud. Instead, she listened, and slipped steadily into pain when Archie talked about the reply he sent to Daisy, since he had promised to call her the next day.

In another week, Archie reported talks with his wife and plans. He had let her make her own decision, and she was back. "She has fixed up her bed in the spare room" he confessed sadly at first, "but she is there after all, and she isn't cross, and she isn't ignoring me."

Honey wondered what Daisy talked about with her husband who had been facing abandonment, or so he thought; but she found she couldn't ask.

GUILTY

After Archie's wife returned, even though she was essentially an invisible influence, there began a new stage in Honey's relationship with Archie.

Honey found there could occasionally be a very bad feeling and it happened especially after she had taken care to be ready and waiting for him, only to receive a late text to tell her he was not coming. A hasty message with nothing in it to comfort her, was a reminder that Daisy existed and actually had prior claim on this man, whom Honey loved and who spent so many hours in her company, assuring her of his love.

Was her sense of unease due to feeling foolish, or guilty? Both? At such times, Honey put on her tracksuit and went running around the town, listening to her music, literally trying to flee from the sickening loneliness coupled with the painful reality she had to deal with.

* * *

Towards the end of July, there arose an opportunity for Honey to travel to the surfing beaches in the Isle of Wight. She would improve her lifesaving skills, attend seminars on subjects relating to fitness through physical activity, and for two weeks she would work alongside other fitness instructors, in a way that would benefit each one who participated. She was thrilled to accept and told Archie about it; feeling sure he would be supportive.

He was. "I think you will have a good time, Honey!" he said. "They'll be lucky to have you there."

He, too, had some news. It seemed Daisy had been working on her health issues and the effects were beginning to show. She had not been so depressed since her return and Archie, who had mentioned once or twice that things were improving, said she was going to weekly meetings of a slimming club, and he felt proud of her.

"Honey, it's you!" he said.

Honey had a moment of intense confusion. "It's me?"

"I have you to thank, for the difference in Daisy!"

She felt herself stiffen. If she was forced to live with the fact that Archie's wife existed – and it was far more obvious now – she certainly did not want to hear too much about her. Archie, oblivious, went on. "You said she must be depressed, so I asked her to see a doctor. She turned out to be clinically ill and there are medicines she can have. They change her frame of mind. Then, the ideas came about keeping fit with good food and exercise. I understand what she is trying to do and I can help her! It's all because of you, Honey!"

It was horribly difficult to accept thanks for this. Her own ideas, her advice, had led to the man she adored being drawn back into his marriage, away from Honey.

* * *

Honey left for her fortnight of recreation and learning, and her feelings were a mixture of excitement and regret. With self-interest at the top of her mind, she was torn. The work experience ahead was enticing, but she knew this could be a sensitive time for her to leave Archie, even though there was really no choice.

You Run Away …

Upon her return, Honey sent a text to Archie and waited for his reply. It came at once, reassuring her that he had been waiting and he longed to see her. Relieved she prepared, dressed in her lace top teamed with a slim chocolate-brown skirt that left her midriff bare. She could not wait to open her door to him, and he walked into the flat with his familiar smile, arms outstretched.

They were every bit as loving as they had always been. He said, however, he could not stay all night and Honey was reminded forcefully that his wife now lived in their home again. She let him go without complaint, feeling that she would have to make sure she did not create a difficult situation for Archie and yet, how difficult *this* was. Honey began to have misgivings in earnest, about leading a life wherein she would remain almost impossibly side-lined. Was she really planning to try? She began to challenge herself.

* * *

A new offer, similar to the work and training in the Isle of Wight, was made to Honey and it was linked with the activities she loved. This time, she would be away from home for much longer than before. Some of her regular classes would be cancelled for the time being, and, where this was not possible, an assistant at the sports centre would cover for her. She would teach fitness in a location in

Newquay. She would have an opportunity to learn how to surf, and she would be part of a select group of trainees with similar qualifications and interests. The position would last for six weeks, starting from halfway through August.

The night before her journey, she shared precious hours with Archie. "What happened to us? What about our song?" he mourned. "You keep going away! You *run away with my heart!*"

* * *

The journey home from Newquay was riotous, since the twenty trainees and tutors who had shared the long break were in high spirits. They travelled back through the country in a specially commissioned coach, which stopped occasionally for coffee breaks or to deliver individuals to their home towns. Everyone was full of energy and wellbeing after spending most of their days in the water – swimming, practising lifesaving, surfing – and on the beaches. Days full of sunshine had extended through September in a true Indian Summer, suntanned faces were all around Honey, and her own typical golden glow had deepened too.

Honey sat beside a blonde-haired young man named Rob, and they shared peanuts and chocolate, and laughed their way through the journey. "We'll keep in touch, won't we?" he asked hopefully, but she shook her head.

"I can't wait to get home, to … to … someone who is waiting …" She wanted to be honest.

Honey had enjoyed her long break, but the golden summer days had passed. She arrived at the flat on a chilly evening. Along with the familiar environment came a flood of intense feelings for Archie. She had missed him and knowing he would soon be there, she felt desperate to see him again.

Some of the work had been demanding, and the break overall was not a holiday, since the activities had been balanced by all kinds of interesting study topics. Honey and her colleagues examined, not just physical fitness and nutritional therapies, but also aspects of psychology, to compliment the work they did overall. Understanding how people showed themselves to be fearful or anxious was especially useful for tutors who would go on to work in settings where swimming (including lifesaving techniques) was taught.

She took a hot shower, and afterwards, dried, refreshed and feeling warmer, she put on a pair of white cotton trousers. They were well-made, with an invisible zip and no creases. She teamed them with a cropped top in a shade of fluorescent orange, and combed her hair. Cut much shorter than before, it looked crisper and more groomed. The style accentuated her cheekbones and beautiful mouth.

Alerted by her messages, Archie was on his way. She closed blinds at the windows of the flat. When he arrived at Honey's door and she opened it, he was already smiling, but his expression changed and he looked nonplussed when she stood there in the doorway.

"Short hair?" he exclaimed. "You look different!" It wasn't a compliment, but the comment got lost in their mutual happiness and Archie wrapped his arms around her with all the same expressions of love as before.

He had a parcel for Honey and when she tore off the wrapping, he pointed to the label. "Fresh fragrance, see Honey?" It was a gift box full of colognes and bath oils, scented with vanilla, lemon and ginger.

They went to bed, hungry for each other, and they were passionate, but while Honey rested later Archie turned his back towards her, and sat on the edge of the bed. He glanced at Honey over his shoulder after a few moments, and she was watching him. Saying nothing, he put on his robe and went into the kitchen, where he began to make coffee.

"Okay?" Honey could see him from her bed. Fresh from her studies, faintly bizarrely, she was aware of his body language. He kept rubbing the side of his nose with two fingers ... he was having doubts.

Archie brought two cups of coffee over to the bedside and set them down, then he knelt on the floor, leaning across the coverlet to take Honey's hands in his own. He sighed, and spoke softly. "Come here."

She shifted until she was closer. He released her hands, and tucked the back of his fingers beneath her chin, lifting it, and he raised his own head a little, so they were looking directly into one another's eyes. "What's the matter?" uneasily she asked. She wondered why he hadn't called her *"Hon'..."*

"Things aren't quite the same, I'm thinking." It was almost a question but not quite, and he spoke the words in a flat tone. Honey was aware of a change now, and it felt alarming. Archie had narrowed his eyes, just fractionally. His expression was composed, and his voice ... well ... Honey thought, it was sort of calm. He closed his lips after speaking, unsmiling.

Her mind raced. *Was* he angry? Does someone speak in a flat voice when they are angry?

During the summer, Honey had indulged in a fling with the handsome, blonde-haired young man named Rob. She thought of it as nothing but fun, part of the experience of being away and something it would be possible to dismiss on her return. She had become so confident in bed; Archie could guess what happened.

She did something that reflected her immaturity. With a little shrug, she said: "Archie, I was away for quite a while." For the second time in their relationship, she intended to indicate almost nothing, but somehow her words acquired a world of meaning, and they were harmful.

He removed his hand from her chin, and stood, abruptly, looking as if he had been slapped. Perhaps she should have denied his statement and said things were *just* the same? Honey was still not mature enough to realise exactly what she needed to say, and in any case, it was already too late to save the situation. Archie's heart instantly relinquished some of his love for her.

"Why is he worrying about that?" Still not fully conversant with the ways of a man, she silently wondered. *"He lives with his wife! I have to accept it, with all that means!"*

She would not say more about Rob. Instead, she told Archie the truth, and in this she was foolish again, because it was ill-timed.

"I love you!"

Archie had expressed his love for Honey many times, and he had waited for her to say she loved him. She had spoken the words he so longed to hear, but he couldn't respond.

In truth, she had no one else in her life. The holiday romance was nothing she cared about; no plans or whispered promises were made with Rob, and Honey had parted from him without regret. This may have disappointed Rob, but Honey had never loved Archie more.

He pulled her against him and tightened his embrace, pressing her head against his shoulder, but his arms were full of tension. He clung, as if he was trying to feel safe. Honey's heart pounded, but it was minutes before he spoke again.

His next words were not what she wanted to hear. "I have to spend more time at home. Daisy depends on me. She did so well, but she still gets rough days."

The intensity of the moments ahead of this information receded, as Honey sought to understand this fresh development. She didn't understand the conversations were linked and Archie, struggling to grasp the change in their relationship, was unable to be transparent. A more experienced woman would have guessed the situation, but Honey was thrown. '... *more time at home?'* Why, exactly? Up until now, while he spent time in the flat, his wife had depended on him in the same way, surely? At least, after she came back to him from her sister's home?

Honey moved to climb out of the bed, slipped her arms into a short robe and went, knotting the belt, to refill her coffee cup. She would not look at Archie. "You know, some women get sure of themselves when they lose weight!" she said. "They feel empowered."

She stopped at that, realising with a shock that her words were hard. She sounded resentful, even spiteful. She remembered how very sad he had been, when nothing he could do was enough to please Daisy or help her recover. She was on the wrong track; Archie's decision was not really about Daisy. He made no reply.

Honey returned to the bedside, where she turned and sat with him, sideways, on the edge of her small bed. He took the cup from her and set it down on the cabinet nearby, before reaching for her hand. He looked very grave, but he lifted her fingertips to his lips, to kiss. She did not pull away, and she tried to hope there would be a way through this sudden sense of shared misery.

RESPONSIBILITY

Honey had celebrated her twenty-seventh birthday while she was in Newquay. She was confident and very beautiful. By this time, she was equipped not only with her degree and several years of experience but also the extra knowledge gleaned from her summer of training. At the sports centre, she began to be given greater responsibilities, with management of the other staff and freedom to make choices in organising class schedules.

When she conducted an outdoor basketball session one afternoon, the excitement of the game and a brisk wind invigorated Honey and her team. Archie turned up at the side of the court, watching. He wore a cap pulled low over his forehead, and a scarf wound around his neck and chin. He had finished his working day earlier than usual. He waited for her to grab her bags before driving her home.

"You shout!" he commented.

"I'm in charge!" she responded, equably.

On this occasion, Archie had taken care to leave the lorry parked away from the sports grounds and Honey noticed this, and also the covering scarf and cap. Although he did not mention a worry, Honey wondered if he had begun to think it was unwise to be seen in her company. Would his wife ever turn up at the gym or in the pool? It seemed a possibility, if Daisy was really getting fitter.

Honey's love for Archie had only deepened, despite the testing times they encountered. Her trip and the episode with Rob felt like nothing of any consequence, compared with the hours spent with Archie, and she was finding it difficult to let him go, each time he had to leave her. Even though her personal strength – both physical and emotional – was not in doubt, the longing to stay by his side never left her.

Knowing he was less unhappy since he was not suffering at home as he had, was perhaps a triumph; but it wrenched at Honey's emotions. Now, Archie was more independent of her love. The changes in his life were not insignificant; Daisy's illness, and her behaviour, had not killed his loyalty and instead of showing any form of resentment, Archie had welcomed his wife and made her return as easy as he could. Honey was not sure, now, that she could make the rest of the world go away for Archie when he came to her; such oblivion was not what he sought, and events had moved with frightening speed, to alter their relationship.

* * *

Honey donned a simple, navy-blue swimsuit, fixed up her hair with combs and made her way to the poolside. She walked with typical grace, straight backed, head up, a confident figure who was genuinely inspirational. The ladies who regularly attended the aqua aerobics sessions tried hard to keep fit, and they aimed to copy Honey, to the best of their ability.

"We have a new girl!" announced one, who was already bobbing about in the water, wearing a plastic cap decorated with fake flowers. "She's quite amazing, really! She lost over five stones!"

A younger woman was sitting on a bench near the pool. She tucked short dark hair behind her ears and adjusted her plastic wristband. "Yes, she's very interesting; I talked to her when she came into Reception," she answered. "We were both early. We had to wait ages …"

She shed a towel from her shoulders and prepared to enter the water, still following her train of thought. "She's been depressed, and she thinks that made her eat too much, so she put on weight." The women nodded in agreement over the vexed question of how *not* to eat for comfort.

Honey was used to overhearing chatter at the start of her classes. Often, there were grumbles about the temperature of the swimming pool. Weight problems were also commonly shared, but Honey would not allow herself to be drawn in, since her advice was now available if a customer paid for an official one-to-one consultation. She paid no attention to their conversation.

Honey slid her long body into the pool, soaked her shoulders for a moment, and then stood, chest-high, to direct her class. She raised her arms with water beading on her skin, and began to demonstrate a method of warming up with twists from the waist. The ladies formed a row facing her, and someone complained that it was hard, doing twists when you were "in water this deep".

The extra member of the group joined them, looking self-conscious. She was a small woman with neat fair hair and bright blue eyes, and she wore a dainty swimming costume, a "tankini", with a pink top teamed with white shorts. She walked cautiously along the poolside, and came to the edge behind Honey, who turned to smile a welcome. She sat down with her feet dangling in the water, then placed her hands on the tiles on either side of her slim hips, and lowered herself into the water. She had a beautiful manicure; her fingers tipped with pink, glossy nails.

Honey found herself briefly examining her own short, squared-off nails, reflecting that she had not painted them for ages! Something important seemed to knock at the back of her mind, but she turned back to the group, and moved on with some bounces. Obeying her instructions then, the group of ladies worked through their routine with enthusiasm, although the flowered hat lady stopped often to rest. "I get breathless!" she told her companions.

"I know how that feels!" said the fair-haired woman, joining in. "I wouldn't even go for a walk, for months!" All of a sudden, she had Honey's full attention. Her next comment made Honey's stomach seem to turn over. "I used to run out of breath, all the time!"

Someone asked, "Have you got a husband, Daisy?" (A nod, and Honey's stomach flipped again.) The same person went on, "What does he think of your weight loss, and this new fitness kick?"

With the honest response that followed, Honey knew the truth. She plunged into an agony of awareness, from which there would be no return.

"He loves it!" Daisy said, and there were smiles from the others. "My skin isn't the best, around my tummy," she told them, frankly. "Archie doesn't mind. He says, I'm lovely!"

* * *

For Honey, much was changing. A special memory, once beautiful, was sullied by Daisy's remarks, and she felt angry and resentful. "My skin isn't the best," the woman said, and Honey's mind jumped back to that hot day when she felt blissfully happy. She remembered Archie's touch, and his words.

"Your skin ... it's sinfully good."

Freed from her awful weight problem, Daisy was far more mobile than before. She was to be seen walking energetically in the park, carrying a bottle of water and carefully checking a stopwatch. When she returned to the next session of aqua aerobics, she had clearly made friends with another group member, the young woman with short dark hair, who often remarked, *"She is really sweet!"*

Honey began to think she might lose her mind.

"I still get a bit wobbly sometimes," Daisy admitted after their swim, referring to her clinical depression. "I can't believe how badly I treated my husband, but it wasn't the real me. I'm just so lucky he spotted that I needed a doctor, to help." She knelt to tie new laces on small white trainers. "I do things like this now," she continued.

"These are my favourite pumps, and I *bothered* to get fresh laces!"

Her friend was right, she was endearing. A narrow gold bracelet shone on one of her wrists. "I even feel younger! I'm never going to let myself go, again!" she vowed.

The End of the Affair

Some cultures seem to embrace and understand the concept of a man who is married also taking a mistress, and it's thought he is able to love both of them. It is sometimes said that the two loves are "different". Honey had considerable self-awareness, but although she knew at the start of their relationship that Archie teased her, she may not have realised how much he loved her for the charm of an *ingenue*. He had respected her, encouraged her to enhance her strength, but perhaps without either of them fully realising it, he enjoyed feeling that he was always in control.

Now, still admiring of Archie and deeply in love, Honey behaved as his equal. More graceful than ever, she adopted a certain confident stance and was no longer childlike, although she continued to be full of fun.

In contrast, Daisy leaned heavily on her husband, trusting and turning to him in a way she hadn't before. She seemed to have shed years along with the pounds, but she remained vulnerable, fearful of the possible return of her depression. Following her achievement of a weight loss, she felt better and more able to take care of herself, but she looked up to Archie, feeling impressed by his guidance, and proud of a recovery process it seemed they'd shared. Daisy was immensely relieved that her husband was willing to go forward, building on that precious recovery, making a fresh start to their marriage.

Archie liked to guide his relationships, and there was beginning to be no doubt that he felt challenged by Honey's positivity and relative independence, at least in terms of her everyday life.

An unwelcome train of thought crossed Honey's mind increasingly often. It had been possible to indulge her love for Archie when he was sad, essentially bereft of the woman he married. Daisy had altered, Archie could not know the outcome of her removal to her sister's home, and she had not given him much hope. Sorrowing, he was a lonely person, who could be deemed to have a right to seek comfort. With Honey, he became animated and happier and she had fallen in love with the funny, emotional and passionate soul he was.

With a wife whom he clearly loved, was rediscovering, and who now shared his home – was he free for Honey to love? Of course, he was not. Many things were being restored to Archie, and Honey was losing ground. "I help her with the food," he confided. "I tell her I listen to cookery shows! I buy tomatoes and chorizo and pasta. I get fruit and make juice for her breakfast!"

"Is he nuts?" Honey wondered helplessly. "He *tells me* all this?"

Archie's behaviour, and his words, were wrecking the trust Honey had built into her perception of him, and sending her into such a state of shock, she could hardly believe what was happening. He did not spot – or care about – the incongruity of their situation, and there was no hiding the fact he liked the more attractive, still dependent Daisy. Then, one day, he returned to their conversation about her potential empowerment. Thankfully, he and Honey were not in bed, but walking along a river bank where Archie asked her to meet him on a Friday evening.

Their way would have been in darkness but for the lights that shone from windows of dwellings that lined the route to their right, and street lamps on the pathway before the houses. Honey and Archie were on a lower track, and an occasional water bird, still wakeful, splashed to their left. They squelched over stones and mud, on an October evening.

Honey had buried her hands inside the pockets of her jeans. Usually, Archie would pull one of them out, to clasp in his own brown fist or tuck beneath his elbow, but this time he seemed content to walk side-by-side, not linked. It wasn't a subtle change. He often waved his hands around when he talked, but he rarely walked beside her without reaching out, in some way. In fact, he tucked both thumbs into his belt, and Honey felt bleak.

Picking up on the point she had made during the evening after her return from America, he wanted to say that his wife was not seeming particularly empowered. "She has many weaknesses. She worries about everything: her age, my work and *my* health too!"

Archie was not speaking wisely, in Honey's opinion. It was impossible to forget how desperately lonely he had been, when Daisy withdrew her conversation, her interest and even her physical presence for so long, and that unhappy time had made him vulnerable. But, if the woman was so fearful, and he loved her, perhaps she should never have lost his fidelity? How had they come to this point? Was it a full circle?

She couldn't force her mind back over so many conversations, so much reflection that followed the times she talked with Archie, or all the feelings that surrounded their relationship. Yet, intrinsic within it, had been his suffering because of the behaviour of his wife – and she, Honey, had supported him!

"You are really strong," he continued, and suddenly she could tell where his speech was heading. "Your strength is inside your head as well as your body, because of your wonderful fitness. I think you … I mean …" It was not something he could bring himself to say but they both knew what he meant.

The unsaid sentence was: *I think, maybe, you are the one who could live without me?*

Honey felt shaken but remained outwardly composed. She

suspected, rationally that she still held a considerable amount of control of the conversation, despite its one-sidedness so far; since he probably hoped for a denial. If she wept at this point and declared herself unable to live without him, soft-hearted Archie would no doubt consent to planning more times together, snatched whenever they could. He would be a man who was prepared to have two women to love and would divide his time, probably even managing to do so fairly effectively!

Honey had readily guessed where she could take the situation next, if she wished. Ahead, there lay the chance of a life in which she did not completely lose Archie, whom she loved. In that awkward scenario, she would have to settle for many hours on her own. Since there was more to her character than practicality, her emotional and womanly responses came into play too, and she knew the choice was not good enough.

It was an opportunity to finish her involvement with a married man, and Honey took it.

* * *

Honey fell into a disastrous state of mind after making her brave decision. Great loss brings unavoidable heartache, and recovery from such grief is a slow process that cannot be escaped or denied.

At first, she tried to go on exactly as normal – except that nothing really felt normal, because there was a huge gap in her life where Archie once was. She continued to take care of herself and jogged to the sports centre each morning, although she left her flat thirty minutes earlier than was her habit, knowing she would feel safer if she made sure not to cross Archie's path. She contrived, each day, to be just as energetic as before, and found that if she left the halls as soon as her classes ended and changed her timing just a little, she did not see Archie at all.

Honey made sure to buy and prepare the food she usually enjoyed, and with her knowledge of nutrition she included in her diet the vitamins which boost energy and mental wellbeing. It was a well-informed approach, and yet she was conscious of feeling forlorn … should she care about what she ate, really? She didn't.

Before long, Honey found she missed Archie so much, the misery overtook everything else in her life and she hardly knew what to do with herself. Her emotions were full of confusion, muddling her thinking. The sensible decision she made, had led to a loss and deep sorrow. She was becoming angry, and began to wonder why she had not handed Archie more blame, and more expressions of that anger. Yet Archie had never lied to her, would even have shown her pictures of Daisy if she had wanted to see them, and in reality, their closeness was founded upon his honest revelations about the unhappiness he felt because of his wife's behaviour and the illness she suffered.

Archie would no doubt have continued to see Honey if she had made that possible. She could have kept him in her life, *if* she had been willing to be side-lined every time Daisy's needs were greater. She felt angry, and could not help it, because he had not chosen her alone.

"I don't even think he really liked my shorter hair," she thought sadly. "What if I tried harder to please him?" Despite the most determined efforts to reject any thoughts of going along with an affair that lasted and would have to be conducted even more secretly than before, Honey found herself pondering, in weaker moments, on ways in which her time and her lifestyle could be managed, so she could see him again. Surely, they would have to be more secretive by far, than they had been when Daisy lived well away from the town?

Could she risk her self-esteem to become the long-term mistress in Archie's life? How would it be, to know that – if Daisy spotted his infidelity – there would certainly follow a terrible time for them all? This train of thought led to a wrestle with her conscience that was like dividing into two different people!

"*No!* I can't live like that!" insisted Honey's moral self, while the part of her that hurt so badly was ready to beg. "Oh, let me! I'm not going to survive ..."

Honey wondered if the times she had accepted as fair enough, the times when she and Archie sat openly together in front of coffee shops in the town's precinct, meant more than she realised. Could it be, Archie was not quite the victim he once seemed? Was he absolutely capable of wanting two women in his life ... not just by chance and in a helpless situation that arose ... but deliberately, needing extra support, refusing to give up on Daisy, and even caring less than Honey had supposed, about the possibility of being found out? This (if true) would change her perceptions significantly. She touched on the idea of facing him with the question, knew she would not get an answer she could believe, knew she would then break her heart over that loss of trust – and threw the idea out.

Relentlessly, she came up against her truest feeling of firm refusal to enter knowingly into a long-term affair, with a man who was definitely planning to stay with his wife. Honey would not try to keep Archie in her life when she knew he had accepted Daisy again and was trying to make her happy – and she would not complicate her thoughts and feelings further, with open anxieties about his intentions so far.

Sadly, she suffered worse than ever, and a sick sense of shame seemed to be part of her honest reflections, making her feel ill. With her strength at a low ebb, Honey was depressed.

RACHEL

It was a dull afternoon in December, when Honey confronted her depression. She struggled through two lessons earlier in the day, encouraging the ladies to be energetic and somehow, she managed to demonstrate how to carry out all her planned exercises. When the group came to the end of the second session and dispersed, Honey normally went to swim alone, purely for pleasure.

On this occasion, she felt a lassitude that led to her pulling a jacket over her light clothing and walking out of doors, where she found a bench and sat, idly watching a squirrel as it collected scraps of food from a rubbish bin. She tried to bear the sorrow that weighed heavily inside her chest as if it was something tangible, drank a little water but left her sandwich, still wrapped, at the bottom of her bag.

At last, Honey returned to the halls, asked one of her team to supervise a later class and walked home to her flat. There was some comfort in opening the door and entering her environment, where she had been happy for so long. The day had grown still more gloomy but a low hum of the central heating system could be heard and Honey closed her blinds, switched on a lamp and boiled a kettle for a hot drink. She regarded her couch with its bright cushions and orange throw, but instead of settling herself there, she wandered aimlessly about the kitchen. She tipped water from her drinking bottle over a cascading spider plant, then carried a mug full of tea to place beside her single bed. She pulled trainers from her feet, shed her jacket and trousers, drew back the soft cream-coloured coverlet, and lay down.

Much later, Honey was woken by the ring of her mobile phone, and took a few moments to locate it. She had left it inside her gym bag and by the time it was retrieved the caller had rung off. Honey examined a list of missed calls.

Rachel answered at once when Honey rang her number, and sounded concerned. "There you are! I tried you several times today! Are you okay?"

"Sorry, Rach'. I wasn't checking my phone …"

"Were you working?"

"Well, yeah, but I'm scared of … I mean, I've told Archie …" Honey got no further and could not stop a great sob from escaping when she contemplated actually *saying* that she had told him not to call or visit her again.

"I'm coming!" Rachel told her. "It will be late but I can leave almost at once! Don't worry Honey!"

The time was seven in the evening and Rachel had a two-hour drive ahead. Honey felt encouraged by the thought that her good friend was on her way. She began to hunt in her kitchen for ingredients she could use to make a meal.

The activity of scrubbing and preparing potatoes for baking, grating cheese, and mixing a salad was helpful, although her mind was apt to wander.

At last, with cooked potatoes filled with a creamy cheese filling keeping warm, the salad piled into a wooden bowl with freshly sliced tomatoes and a scattering of feta cheese; a good aroma of hot coffee filled the flat, and Honey considered her preparations were complete. She poured herself a small glass of white wine, changed into a sweatshirt and a pair of jeans, rubbed lemon fragranced lotion into her hands, and combed her hair.

Without wanting to remember why she was thinking of it, she hunted in a drawer for an emery board and a tiny bottle of pink nail varnish; then she found a film to watch on her laptop, sat amongst the cushions in her sofa and made her fingernails look pretty.

At nine o'clock exactly, there came a knock and Rachel was there. She held out her arms to her friend as soon as the door was opened, and hugged Honey very tightly.

* * *

Rachel produced a pair of pale green pyjamas from her holdall, and also a bottle of brandy. She would stay, she said, "all night *and all tomorrow!*" Honey didn't argue.

They ate the food that Honey had prepared, sitting together on the couch with their plates on their knees. "I like these squashed-up potatoes!" remarked Rachel.

"Crushed …" Honey corrected her, smiling. It was her first proper smile for some time, and the meal was the only hot food she had prepared all week, she confessed, finding it much easier to enjoy her food in the presence of her friend. They watched the last part of the film together, and Rachel said she didn't need to see it from the start, it was one of her favourites and she could say all the words if Honey wanted her to … With this offer politely declined, they enjoyed it together. Having eaten, they piled their dishes and cutlery into the sink, made fresh coffee then poured brandy into small glasses, to drink with it.

The two young women had been friends for many years, and they knew one another well. Sipping drinks, they talked about their work at first, and Honey described her extra training trips, and Rachel took an interest, because her own job as a physical education instructor in a secondary school had similarities.

At last, they both got into the single bed. It was not too difficult to share, as neither one of them was very wide – in fact, Rachel was truly dainty. They plumped pillows and lay propped up, as Honey talked about Archie and found herself describing as much as she could remember of their first meeting, the apparently casual times when they chatted following it, and the way the feeling that they were soul mates developed and at last overtook any fears of acting foolishly.

Rachel took her friend's hand and examined her pink nail varnish, rubbing the painted fingernails with her own thumb, reflectively. "I'm a bit hung up on that part where you got in the lorry in the first place," she confessed. "I mean, doesn't it feel like something you wouldn't normally do?"

Yes, Honey knew it had been a bad move, and she had tried to push that thought aside quite often. If she had simply waved Archie away that day, she might have avoided any sort of acknowledgement after that, and nothing would ever have happened between them. She had been impulsive. She reminded Rachel that she had hurt her foot at the time, and was a bit stuck.

Rachel was determined not to add to her friend's unhappiness, but she was moved and alarmed by the story. Some fear that Honey could try to go forward without spotting how many mistakes she had made, knocked at her mind, and she persisted, as gently as she could. "When you went to meet him that first time, Hon' ... what did you think was behind his "more to say" comment? You weren't getting a heads-up to something a bit deep?"

Honey *had* wondered at herself even at the time, waiting for him, thinking he looked older, buying ice cream in an action that was strangely disconnected from her usual habits. She remembered that odd defensiveness when Archie exclaimed "I knew you'd wait!" and she had felt irritated by his assumption.

She said, "I think I sort of wanted to prove to myself, that I could get free of stupid Simon! You know? Stop letting him make me feel like I couldn't trust anyone at all."

At that, Rachel had to hide a tear. Honey didn't see it, and she went on explaining that, as she learned of his situation and the picture unfolded, Archie's unhappiness had made a difference to her feelings; he was vulnerable, and had not felt like a threat. Honey wanted Rachel to understand he had seemed a kind and genuine man; and she still firmly believed the truth of this.

Rachel listened carefully, and drew her own conclusions. Wisely, she did not offer too much comment. In fact, her friend was definitely struggling with self-reproach. When Honey asked forlornly, "Why do you think I did all that? I feel ashamed! I remember what happened but I don't feel like I know why …" Rachel knew it was best to be supportive.

She was firm. "It was just because of love. Don't try to work it out, Hon'. Probably, you will always love him."

"Mm," Honey accepted this. "I kind of like it that I will … I haven't, you know, turned against him, even though I feel so hurt." She had made a decision. "This will *never* happen again!"

Before they fell asleep, Rachel had a comforting point to make. "One day, all this will go more like a story. Part of your life, that you can bear again, when you think about the good times."

"Thanks Rach', so clever …" Honey murmured sleepily. "Wisdom …" she turned over and settled down more comfortably. "You've got the *wisdom of Job!*"

* * *

From force of habit Rachel awoke at six o'clock. Honey slept on, even though her friend scrambled across her to climb out of the narrow bed. Rachel began to make herself busy. She kept the blinds closed and switched on a lamp in the kitchen area of the open plan flat. She filled the kettle, boiled it and made a mug of tea which she took with her into the bathroom, where she showered, shamelessly plundering a luxurious quantity of orange-scented gel. She found a chunky, wide-tooth comb and tidied her short red-gold hair with it, a little clumsily.

Still wrapped in a towel, she returned to the kitchen and removed and stacked all the crockery they had left in the sink the night before. She finished her tea and added the empty mug to the pile of dishes, filled a red plastic bowl with steaming water and soap bubbles, and began to wash up. Inevitably, Rachel was thinking about her friend.

When Honey finally decided to leave her mother and stepfather in the little house which Simon tainted so badly for her, there was a stark reason and Rachel knew the full truth behind the brave decision. The man was unsafe around Honey. His sarcasm was nothing but a front, designed to make the overall impression one of contempt but in reality, he had trouble keeping his hands off the eighteen-year-old girl.

Rachel knew Honey observed her mother's dependency, feared she would not be believed if she talked about Simon's behaviour and hoped that – left alone with him – Linda's love would evaporate. Almost eight years had passed and this had not happened. It was surely very tough for Honey that she could rarely spend time with her mother.

Hunting in cupboard drawers, she found neatly folded tea towels, took a blue-and-white checked one, and began to dry the clean things, finding places for cutlery and bowls in cupboards and leaving a few plates stacked tidily on the counter. At length, feeling chilly, she discarded her bath towel, and pulled some clothes from her overnight bag. Over modest white underwear she put on a loose grey dress and a short green cardigan. She put a hand on a radiator to check it was switched on and, for good measure, took the throw from the sofa and tucked it across Honey's shoulders.

Rachel found a fruit bowl, deliberated and chose a banana. Eating, she sat by Honey, watching her sleep in her pretty bed, thinking fondly that she looked ethereal. "Like an angel, an *earth angel* – not just sort of floaty but with strength!"

What a difference there must have been, between the poorly wife with her dreadful weight and mental health issues, and her downheartedness, and the exquisite younger woman who smiled often, and whose great passions were health and fitness. Polar opposites.

She considered her friend had been ill-used. Daisy left Archie and moved away for a long time, and without Honey's love and steadfast patience, he would have been very lonely. It seemed he had enjoyed her company and grasped the opportunity of having an affair. The two of them had a powerful mutual attraction, and understanding, but you couldn't discount the effect of Honey's fabulous looks. Attractive though he clearly was (and he sounded sweet and passionate), surely Archie had a misplaced sense of morality?

Of course, if he *was* fundamentally moral, he must have hated the fact that Honey had a fling when she went away. No matter that it was brief or that Honey herself thought little of it – Archie's pride must have taken a serious knock. Rachel wondered if it was a pity her friend was not a better liar! If Archie had not realised there had been another man in Honey's life, perhaps he would have clung tighter. And yet, she was not sure that was the best outcome for her friend.

Honey still wanted to believe that Archie was fundamentally a good man, and thought he had probably chosen Daisy over herself from a sense of duty, as well as the love he had always admitted to. This, Honey believed; even though she was not unaware that he would almost certainly have kept her in his life if she had been will-ing to accept being side-lined whenever Daisy's needs took prece-dence.

Rachel suspected Archie's feelings had altered drastically with the news of her friend's sexual encounter during her trip away in Newquay. He had hardened, weighed up his options, and had not been able to maintain an entirely loving front. He would have set-tled for a wife *and* a mistress, was able to settle for a wife alone – would not settle for Honey exclusively.

It seemed quite possible that, in time, he would again struggle to cope with his self-centred wife, who had created such unhappiness for him before she changed her mind, expecting him to be waiting for her. Perhaps one day, he would feel ill-used again, and do his best to come back to the sweet, proud young woman whom he thought he could live without?

POSTSCRIPT

(Denial Anger Bargaining Depression ... Acceptance)

Honey visited her mother just ahead of the twenty-fifth of December, on a day when she knew Simon was not at home. Linda made her welcome, showed her a small, fragrant Christmas tree smothered in silver and golden baubles and tiny fairy lights, and had some wrapped gifts ready to give her when she left. They went shopping and treated themselves to a lunch in a small bistro, where they ate hot quiche and drank white wine. Honey chose not to confide in her mother; she never did, but they enjoyed one another's company for several precious hours.

She was invited to spend time with Rachel and her family on New Year's Eve, and accepted, staying for an afternoon and one night, not wanting to intrude. Otherwise, she kept herself busy, and cosy when she was in her flat.

In January, Honey moved on in a characteristically determined way, but ordinary life continued to be tough while she followed similar patterns each day to those when, for so long, she was sharing time with Archie. Gradually, often feeling as if she hauled herself forward, she went on altering her lifestyle in all the ways she could. Her discussion with Rachel had helped her recover a sense of personal strength. She would rid herself of the guilty feelings which had threatened to engulf her with a frightening new anxiety about leaving the flat, and an oddly physical, sick response too.

At first, it was not difficult to abandon the local newsagent's kiosk; going there was just a habit, and it was possible to make a change. She began to buy water and snacks from the vending machines at the sports halls.

Honey used some of her savings to buy a small car. She had her driver's licence, and possessing her own vehicle was such fun, she found herself wondering why she hadn't treated herself sooner. Once at the centre, she used a private parking space to the rear and could dash inside through a private door. With returning energy, she began to spend an extra thirty minutes on a treadmill before classes began, to make up for the time that used to be well-used in the exercise of jogging to work ... when Archie did not drive her there in his lorry.

The greatest difference Honey could make, was to move away from the area of the pretty precinct near her flat, with its fountain and coffee shops, and the kiosk. This was accomplished quite swiftly with the help of a member of her team, who identified a vacant flat on the other side of the town. Removed from the places she had loved, Honey found solace when she looked through her windows in the early mornings. When winter began to pass and days became lighter, baby squirrels played in a coppice of fir trees across the road outside, and diminutive muntjac deer grazed. The contented cooing of pigeons was restful, and before long Honey liked her new home just as much as the old.

She found a cheerful neighbour, a motherly lady named Irene, who liked to share a chat. Honey invited her to visit and drink tea, and enjoyed making the new flat clean and welcoming. Good-natured Irene was happy to be invited, and she brought a cactus in a small yellow pot as a housewarming present. In turn, she received a snippet from the spider plant, and was delighted when Honey offered to exercise her elderly terrier. With black-and-white "Patch" happy to share her walks, Honey would make her way along wood-land pathways, which she accessed by climbing a stile, with the dog

under her arm, after they crossed a narrow road in front of the
block of flats.

When she felt ready to jog again, a route to the sports hall took
Honey along a track flanked by tall trees. The way meandered
along, behind the rear gardens of rows of houses, to emerge onto
the wide pathway she knew so well. There, she could increase her
pace for a few moments and arrive at the area in front of the building in no time. Jogging, she wore her headphones, listened to
upbeat music and let her eyes glaze over her surroundings, only
making sure she was headed in the right direction. When rainy
weather made the track muddy, Honey often used a longer stretch
of the more familiar route. She wore a boyish cap, black, with the
peak drawn down low over her brow. She ran purposefully with her
chin down, and made up her mind to ignore passing traffic.

Honey put a new instructor in charge of the classes which Daisy
attended. In her managerial role, it was not difficult to check book-
ings in her private office, and ensure her timetable kept her away
from the entrance and reception areas when she knew the older
woman – with her somewhat incongruous childish air – was there.

In this careful way, Honey conducted her life without Archie,
and it was fulfilling again. She even accepted an invitation from
Irene's shy, fair-haired grandson and they giggled together over a
silly film. Recently graduated from university, James was around
three years younger than Honey. She liked his gentle deference, and
discovered he shared her love of swimming.

* * *

Honey let her hair grow longer, and added silvery highlights. She
kept her fingernails short, and painted with the matt ivory shade
she preferred. She drove her car sometimes, ran often and went every
Sunday to swim with James, and when the weather became warmer,
they travelled a few miles to a nearby beach. Its shore was stony but
they could enjoy a swim in the sea and afterwards walk together to

eat fresh fish, fried while they waited in a restaurant that was little more than a shack, where the owner brought warm rolls to their table, and wine in a carafe.

* * *

Honey had worked her way, dragging her feet, through the stages of grief and arrived at "acceptance". Sadly, as every bereft person knows in their heart, when sorrow is honestly unbearable the stage of acceptance never truly comes to stay, no matter what counsellors and therapists would have us believe. It becomes possible to go on, somehow, but the greater one's emotional intelligence, the more acute is the pain.

Honey confessed to no-one, not even kind-hearted Rachel, that she had to live with longing. She knew she would be safe from her feelings only if Archie never, ever confronted her again.

FIN

And ... know that man doth not live by bread only, but by every word that proceedeth out of the mouth of the Lord ...

Deuteronomy 8:3 (King James Bible)

THEIR SONG

The Calling – Wherever You Will Go

If you would like to send feedback to the author, please do! lisaskeet@live.co.uk

Review Requested:
We'd like to know if you enjoyed the book. Please consider leaving a review on the platform from which you purchased the book.

Lightning Source UK Ltd.
Milton Keynes UK
UKHW010412130122
397052UK00009B/389/J